LUPO

AND THE CURSE AT BUCKINGHAM PALACE

LUPO

AND THE CURSE AT BUCKINGHAM PALACE

ABY KING

Illustrated by Sam Usher

Hodder
Children's
Books

A division of Hachette Children's Group

First published in Great Britain in 2015
by Hodder Children's Books

1

A Catalogue record for this book is available from the British Library

ISBN: 978 1 444 92152 6

Typeset in Egyptian 505 BT Light by Avon DataSet Ltd,
Bidford-on-Avon, Warwickshire

Printed and bound by Clays Ltd, St Ives plc

Hodder Children's Books
a division of Hachette Children's Group
Part of Hodder & Stoughton
Carmelite House
50 Victoria Embankment, London EC4Y 0DZ
An Hachette UK company

www.hachette.co.uk
www.theadventuresoflupo.com

For my family

From Berrimans and Bielefeld to
Buckingham Palace
and beyond . . .

Contents

Lupo glimpsed the picture on the front page of the Duke's newspaper. It was a black and white photograph of the Queen smiling in front of Buckingham Palace. Alongside her was a large telescope pointed up at the moon. It was nearly suppertime. Lupo's stomach groaned loudly, distracting him. He rolled on to his back, exposing a freckly pink underbelly so that Prince George could tickle him affectionately.

The Duchess was sitting on a smart red sofa in the middle of the living room, putting the finishing touches to a letter she was writing on Kensington Palace paper. Sealing the envelope, she said, "The Queen's Birthday and the eclipse will be a special day tomorrow. So I think early to bed for everyone, especially since Daddy is on night feeding duty tonight!" She walked over to her husband, the Duke, who carefully handed her the new baby. Prince George was a toddler and Lupo loved playing with him. They both looked forward to the day when they could play with the baby that seemed to have the whole world whipped up in a frenzy of love and excitement.

As the Duchess took the baby from her husband's arms, she looked down at the newspaper next to him. "What are you reading, darling?" she asked.

"It's an article about Prince Bertie's journals. They've been missing for over a hundred years! But it says here in today's paper that they have been found at Buckingham Palace. My . . . my . . . incredible. I looked everywhere for them when I was young because my grandfather told me that they contained the story of a lost family mystery, an Egyptian curse and an ancient cat."

Lupo's long black tail began to wag. It bumped against the Duke's feet. The words "Buckingham Palace", "curse" and "ancient cat" heightened his doggy senses, sending them into overdrive. He scratched his left ear. It had been a while since his last adventure, but he'd never had one at Buckingham

Palace and yearned to explore the mysterious royal residence with its many secretive trap doors, tunnels and staircases.

He bowed down at Prince George's little feet. "Buckingham Palace, George – did you hear that? Oh, if only Holly was here – it's been ages since I was at the Palace. I do like visiting her there." Unable to hide his affections for the Queen's most loyal corgi, Lupo twisted on to his back and smiled, revealing his soft little teeth.

George *gooed* into Lupo's face, "Bucking-jam-Poo-lace!" They both fell into fits of giggles.

The Duchess yawned loudly whilst cradling her little baby. "A curse at Buckingham Palace? What's next? Secret tunnels underneath it?"

Lupo's ears pricked up in recognition. The Duchess couldn't have known how right she was. Lupo had known about the lost passages since he was a puppy. He had even used one of them known as the Blue route to travel to Windsor Castle on one of his previous adventures. The Red route – which ran directly under Apartment 1A – remained unexplored by him. The short passage between Kensington Palace and Buckingham Palace had originally been

3

designed as a tunnel for Queen Victoria but now it was used by ghosts and mice. It was sumptuously decorated and ran right under Buckingham Palace's tall brick walls and behind the royal police guards. Lupo knew it had been hundreds of years since any human had wandered through the passages.

Nanny appeared, offering to take the baby to give the Duchess a chance to finish making dinner.

I wonder what Holly is having for dinner? Lupo thought. One day, I hope I'll have a good excuse to use the Red route. Her Majesty's dogs stopped him from visiting Holly, and he dared not be caught using one of the secret entrances to Buckingham Palace by Monty, Willow or Candy. The royal corgis kept their distance whenever he was at their grand residence. When he visited with the Duke he would see them muttering in corners and turning their noses up at his relaxed, friendly spaniel gestures of goodwill. Vulcan, the Queen's dorgi, was far worse – he seemed to make it his mission in life to get Lupo into all sorts of trouble. Only Holly had welcomed him and helped him settle into his royal life.

Prince George was restless, so started pulling on Lupo's long black ears for attention. Distracted by thoughts of Holly, Lupo said, "The things Holly must see in that Palace, George!" He barked softly. "I'll bet she knows all about the lost treasures and forgotten mysteries!" His tail flicked happily in the air as a shudder of excitement tingled down his dark back and his long, tangled black ears twitched, eager for more of the Duke's story.

The Duchess saw the excitement in the royal spaniel's eyes. "The missing journal of an old prince? Sounds like a good story. I think you should tell George and Lupo all about Prince Bertie whilst I feed and change this little one."

Letting the paper flop over his large, comforting hands the Duke answered, "Good idea. Oh hang on, boys, before I begin . . . I will warn you that this story's ending is yet to be revealed. Perhaps now that the journals have been found, the mystery may finally be solved."

The Duke put down his newspaper. "Let's begin at the beginning and worry about the curse, the ancient cat, and Buckingham Palace later," he said. "*This* story starts when Queen Victoria decided to send her eldest son, Prince Bertie, on an official tour of Egypt."

Lupo's heart began beating faster. He had learned about Queen Victoria and Egypt in his history lessons with Herbert, the smart brown mouse who was the Head of Mice Intelligence Section 5. He breathed in deeply and sniffed the big, yellowing globe at the far end of the room. The mere idea of the world beyond Kensington Palace filled him with a yearning to explore. As a young pup he and Herbert had spent entire lessons turning the globe, studying the different continents. Though he had never been there, he knew exactly where Egypt was.

Prince George whispered into the royal dog's big black ear, "*E-pit! Yippee!*"

Lupo replied in the secret language that only the two of them could understand – a language of *sniffs*, *chomps* and *licks*. *Sniffing* loudly through his wet, black nose, he said: "An ancient story!"

George settled as close as he could to Lupo's warm soft body and promptly stuck his thumb in his mouth. He curled his princely fingers around the spaniel's ears for comfort.

"Bertie was a very adventurous prince," said the Duke. "He was the first prince of England to do an official tour of the ancient world, its

6

pyramids and the Valley of the Kings."

George asked Lupo what a pyramid was by blowing bubbles and *squirming* a lot. Lupo replied by licking the side of his face and *sniffing* loudly into his ear. "Herbert told me it was a big pile of old bricks," he said. George pointed to his Lego and Lupo nodded.

Patting Lupo's head, the Duke continued, "Oh and Bertie had a terrier, not a scruffy royal cocker spaniel like you!"

Lupo smiled proudly.

"Bertie left England on a royal ship," said the Duke. "It was a long and dangerous journey. To pass the time he read to his dog and learned all about ancient Egypt. He wrote daily in his incredible journals, which he planned to give to his mother on his return.

"Much to Bertie's and his dog's relief, they finally arrived in Egypt's hot and dusty capital, Cairo. The moon hung heavily on that first night. Whilst the Egyptians huddled around a large fire and spoke of curses, the Prince lay awake, unable to sleep. He was too excited. In the morning the royal group would be leaving for the Pyramids, travelling by boat down the River Nile. They were headed for the Valley of the Kings!"

George stuck his finger in Lupo's ear and *mumbled*, "E-pit Kings!"

Lupo shook his head, dislodging the toddler's finger. "They weren't called kings back then. They were called pharaohs!"

George tried to stick his finger back in Lupo's ear, and *groaned*. "One day I will be a pharaoh and a king!" He pointed up to his father and giggled.

The Duke attempted to show them all how the ancient Egyptians walked. His long arms zigzagged together as he walked along with his knees bent.

"All the great pharaohs were found in the Valley of the Kings, George," he said. "They were buried in big tombs with the wealth of Egypt! But some of the pharaohs' tombs were protected by terrible curses."

Lupo growled playfully and George giggled as the Duke bashed his knee on a side table.

"Prince Bertie decided to take a sneak peek. He scooped up his terrier, and snuck out of the camp in the dead of night."

George *waved* his little hands in the air and

grumbled, "I want to go to E-pit with Lupo! I want to see the pyramids!"

Lupo *panted* and *scratched* at the floor, saying: "George, there are still lots of mummies in the pyramids! Can you imagine them trying to find a way out, fast asleep but walking around like zombies?"

George jumped up and down *gurgling* merrily. He reached out with both arms to the Duchess. She returned with the baby once again asleep in her arms. "Mummy!"

The Duchess bent down to George and kissed the top of his head. George waved at the sleeping baby and then put his thumb back in his mouth and resumed stroking Lupo's velvety nose.

"At the big pyramids, Bertie found a camel and headed out of the city and into the desert." The Duke waved his big hands across their faces. "Thick clouds covered the moon. Bertie watched as it totally disappeared! All of a sudden the air turned thick and there was a strange rumbling."

Mystified, the Duchess looked down at them.

"Bertie was surrounded by swirling sand. IT WAS A SANDSTORM!" explained the Duke.

George and Lupo both began *blowing* and *panting*

9

as if they too were lost in the sandstorm.

"The sand was in his eyes and throat and covered his clothes. He needed to take shelter! The camel pushed through the storm, carrying the brave but fearful Bertie. Finally they came upon an entrance to a cave. Bertie and his dog crawled in, relieved to be out of the perilous storm.

"Inside the cave, they began to explore. They travelled deep into the heart of it. It was cold but fortunately the Prince was prepared and had enough matches on him to start a fire."

The Duchess excused herself, saying that supper needed her attention. Lupo and George didn't move a muscle. They had crawled under the oversized cream sofa, imagining they too were in a dark, ancient cave. Only their faces stuck out so that they could carry on watching the Duke. George *grumbled* and *blinked* several times in the darkness. Lupo moved closer, keeping the young heir warm, his tail resting on top of the prince's pink toes.

"This is the bit of the story I love the most," continued the Duke. "As the flames from the little fire grew, Bertie saw more clearly where he was. It wasn't a cave at all. He was in a tomb! Except this was no ordinary tomb. It wasn't a *human* tomb! The walls were covered in paintings of animals dancing, running and playing in the sunshine. Its floor was painted to look just like the sea!

Bertie sank lower to get a closer look. He saw fish made from silver darting amongst blue sapphire dolphins who were rolling in the water with stone whales. Bertie's terrier jumped on to the back of a giant turtle that was bobbing along the top. It was all so real that when the crafty dog tried to jump in and swim along he got a bit of a shock! When the Prince rested his hand on the head of a snapping green crocodile the little dog barked wildly!"

George stroked Lupo's nose. "SNAP! SNAP!" he *gurgled*.

"Flames from the fire flickered all around the walls and they lit up the paintings. Bertie saw tigers hiding in grasslands, stalking grey elephants which were rampaging through hand-drawn mountains. Below them were antelope, prancing in and out of a yellow meadow, and brown monkeys swinging on windblown trees!"

The Duke was pretending to investigate the cave but the living room was no match for the painted tomb. He said, "A door at the far end of the tomb was covered in hieroglyphics. It warned of a terrible curse."

Chomp, *chomp*, *sniff* said Lupo, totally overwhelmed. "OH NO, THE CURSE, GEORGE! *DON'T GO IN, BERTIE!* STOP!"

"Bertie pushed open the door to the inner sanctum, breaking the sacred seals!"

"NO!" said George, and Lupo barked.

"Bertie found himself in a room filled with ancient treasure . . . BUT!" the Duke cried, causing both Lupo and George to jump with fear under the sofa, "guarding the treasure were several sphinx statues surrounding a solid gold tomb belonging to a CAT!"

Lupo imagined the stone sphinxes arranged like George's toy soldiers. He made a low growl as his tail helicoptered round and round. He cocked his head to the left.

"George, I don't like the sound of this: Herbert once told me that sphinxes were the soldiers of Egypt's highest-born pharaohs. So it's odd that they would be protecting a cat! I don't think Herbert ever mentioned an animal tomb before? As for the curse . . . this really is a mystery."

George "meowed" – something he only ever normally did whenever he saw Kitty, the Kensington Palace tabby. "Pussy cat, pussy cat!"

The Duke looked down at his son who was gently stroking Lupo's fur. "Bertie was surprised to see that instead of a traditional ancient pharaoh death mask, there was a solid gold mask of a cat. It had to be a very important cat because it was wearing a pharaoh's crown and was clutching the sceptre and rattle that belonged to the ruler of Egypt. Bertie felt a chill on the back of his neck – he could feel the sphinx's stony eyes watching his every move."

George lifted up one of Lupo's paws and tried to hide underneath it, *grumbling*. "Hide!"

"Don't worry, buddy," said Lupo with a reassuring wink. "I'll protect you!"

The Duke leaned into the edge of the sofa. Lupo and George waited with baited breath.

"Bertie decided to open the cat's tomb."

Lupo looked wide eyed to George. "OH NO! Everyone knows you can't disturb a sleeping cat!" Sensing danger he *barked furiously*.

"It's all right, Lupo," said the Duke. "Bertie wasn't afraid. Like you, he wasn't afraid of anything."

The Duke suddenly grew more serious. "Something must have stopped him in his tracks. Maybe it was the ancient curse? Perhaps it was the hieroglyphics that warned of a terrible curse?"

George didn't understand what hieroglyphics were so he screwed up his face. The Duke tried to explain but it made George even more confused. So Lupo tried. He *wriggled* and *scratched*. "They're strange shapes of animals." He finished his description in a series of short whines whilst pointing at Prince George's Mother's Day picture on the mantelpiece. George *burbled* happily as he finally understood.

"You see, the tomb was cursed. Do you want to know what the curse said?" The two explorers under the sofa nodded slowly in silence, so the Duke explained: "HE WHO ENTERS, HE WHO WAKES ME, SHALL SUFFER THE CURSE OF A DREAMLESS SLEEP."

George stuck out his bottom lip and crawled out from under the sofa, wanting a cuddle from his daddy.

The Duchess returned to the room with Nanny cradling the baby. She handed her husband a glass of water. "Darling, you are getting everyone very wound up, right before we eat. Come on, Nanny, let's leave them to it. The lamb is nearly done but I might need your help with the potatoes if that's all right."

"I'm nearly finished," said the Duke, giving Prince George a big hug. "Bertie and his dog left the cave when the storm passed. Thirsty and tired, they finally got back to camp to a hero's welcome. Everyone was relieved to see Bertie safely back," said the Duke, glugging down the water.

Lupo *bounced* around, *yelping*, "Tell us about the curse! What happened to the CAT?" But it was no good – only George understood what the *panting*, *sniffing* and *whining* meant.

George responded by blowing a big round bubble with his spit, which meant he was hungry.

The Duke put down the empty glass, his thirst quenched. "Bertie returned to the cave with his servants and had all the treasure packed up and shipped back to England, in a box labelled 'Private, for Her Majesty the Queen's Eyes Only.'"

Seeing his son yawning, the Duke skipped to the end of the story. "Now comes the mystery. The treasure was never seen again."

Lupo's ears lifted and he cocked his head to one

side, thinking to himself, Now that really *is* a mystery.

"Some say that Queen Victoria was terrified of cats! When she read about the cat's curse she had all the boxes from the strange tomb thrown into the Thames! Others say she locked the entire contents of the tomb into a hidden room at Buckingham Palace. But no one has ever seen the strange cat's sarcophagus and her treasure was lost for good!" The Duke saw George's eyes growing more sleepy. "And what of the curse . . . ? Well, Bertie never slept properly ever again! His dreams were filled with visions of a deathly ancient cat."

With that, the Duke fell silent, as if lost in thought. But Lupo was transfixed.

The Duchess called out from the kitchen disturbing the uneasy peace. Lupo could smell the lovingly made supper, the Duke's favourite.

"I think that's enough," she said. "Bertie's adventures were a very long time ago." The Duke's stomach groaned. "Now, who's hungry?"

1
A Troublesome Cat

The Duke left the room carrying Prince George, who was once again *meowing*. He'd seen Kitty sitting next to the globe at the far end of the room. Kitty was Lupo's friend, even though she was a cat. Lupo waited until he saw father and son walk down the corridor towards the kitchen before he said: "Kitty, I *know* you are in here. I saw you sneak in earlier."

The pretty tabby came out from behind the sofa, curling her lithe frame around an old lamp table. She stopped to look out of the window and up at the early evening stars. Finally she spoke. "Do you believe the story, Lupo? Do you think Prince Bertie really did find a cursed cat tomb in the desert?"

"Of course!" Lupo replied, noticing how her long thin tail was curling up and down, something she did when she was upset. "Kitty, your tail . . . it's curling."

Immediately Kitty stopped the tell-tale tail with her left paw. She gazed hard at the moon and changed the subject. "It looks so bright tonight. The kind of night where one could get lost for a while." She blinked twice and then looked at the floor, standing perfectly still as if she was putting a puzzle together in her mind. When she was done thinking, she said, "The eclipse is tomorrow, huh?"

Lupo raised his eyebrow, suspicious of Kitty's behaviour. The palace cat was stubborn and as mysterious as the moon itself. He walked over to her at the window and stood beside her, looking up at the moon playing peek-a-boo with some dark clouds.

"Yes, it's going to be something all right," he said. "A total solar eclipse! Herbert told me that the moon will pass between the sun and the Earth, and that it will block the sun out completely! Everything will turn to darkness. But we need not panic – the sun will come back. Spooky, though! I think the Queen's birthday this year will be like no other."

Kitty seemed lost in her thoughts. A star whizzed across the sky. "Did you see that?" said Lupo. "It was a comet. Quick, make a wish!" He squeezed his eyes closed. When he opened them Kitty blinked and said, "Remember, you can't tell me what you wished for or else it won't come true."

Lupo nodded quietly. "OK. But one day, I will." His tummy was rumbling loudly as the smell of the Duchess's cooking wafted into the room, tickling his black nose.

Kitty put a paw on Lupo just as he was about to head out to the kitchen, stopping him in his tracks. "Wait, Lupo! There is something I have to tell you. I think the eclipse is a bad sign." She saw a flash of concern cross his kind spaniel face. "What I mean to say is . . . won't it be odd to see the sun disappearing and it be night-time all of a sudden?"

"Is that what's bothering you?" Lupo asked. Kitty nodded. "Don't be frightened. Look, I was thinking it might be cool to check it out from the attic. The palace ghosts are all up for seeing it, too. They want to use the eclipse to scare all the palace visitors away in the middle of the day by gliding down the main staircase! Now what's so bad about that? Why don't you come and watch it with me?"

Kitty smiled meekly. "That's nice of you to ask me, Lupo. But I don't know if I will be back in time for it. I have to go and visit my Aunt Matilda." The palace cat jumped on to the Duchess's special armchair. Then, because she wanted to warn Lupo without scaring him before she left she said, "Lupo, I don't think that Prince Bertie just stumbled into any old tomb. It's possible he found Ebony."

"Ebony?" Lupo asked.

"Yes, that was her name. My aunt Matilda used to tell me a bedtime story about an ancient Egyptian cat called Ebony!" She turned her head and flashed her green eyes. "If Bertie found her tomb, then it's proof that she was real. Those journals could lead the way to the missing evidence of her existence. Ebony would no longer be just some bedtime story! Everything she was – she did – no longer lost to the sands of time."

Lupo furrowed his shaggy brows, confused as to why Kitty seemed to be so worried about the Duke's story.

She tried to explain, "Lupo. Don't you see? It's the curse . . ."

"The curse? What about it?" he dared ask.

She purred a rhythmic beat and then, knowing she had said too much, turned her gaze back to the pale moon. "I must go. Before it's too late."

"Lupo?" called the Duke. "Supper!" Lupo looked towards the kitchen. "Lupo! Come!" shouted the Duchess.

When he turned back Kitty was gone.

Prince George was fast asleep under his toy wombat in his cot within the nursery at Kensington Palace. A night-light glowed softly in the corner. Its light sent animal shapes spiralling around the walls. Lupo watched the playful shadows from under the cot. He was unable to settle.

After tucking into his bowl of leftover supper, he had decided to see if he could find Kitty. He had hoped that she was asleep in George's uncle's room. But when he got to Apartment 3, Kensington Palace, all he could find was a load of dirty sports clothes spilling out of the same laundry basket Kitty called her bed. No tabby cat anywhere to be found.

He poked his head around the many doors throughout Kensington Palace, trying to find her. He walked down corridors and looked in the hiding holes Queen Victoria had used in the hope he may locate his friend, but the only animals he found were palace mice, who were busy racing along the hallways, which thronged with tourists during the day but were unused at night. He stopped briefly to marvel as a group of mice got to work mending the worn edges of a red carpet. Lupo watched as they pulled off loose threads and carefully rolled them up for future use elsewhere, all the while singing together as they toiled.

A tiny bat flew in through an open window and down the corridor, heading for its home in the attic. Lupo hoped that it was a sign that Kitty was roaming around. Most of the palace animals tended to flee when they saw her coming. The palace cat stalked any animals that she felt didn't belong inside Kensington's royal residence.

Unable to track her smell, Lupo yawned. It was late. An MI5 security mouse scurried past. Lupo thought of his friend Herbert who had the answers to most things.

He made his way back to the nursery via Nanny's room. Looking in, there was no sign of Kitty. Nanny was knitting a blue hat in front of a late night Spanish soap opera. As he approached the nursery, he listened outside the Duke and Duchess's bedroom, only to find that the Duke was fast asleep and the Duchess was feeding the baby in an old rocking chair. He'd missed his opportunity for an affectionate good night cuddle with the snoring Duke.

Lupo shimmied back under the big white cot and turned several times before finding the perfect spot. Resting his nose on his black paw, he blinked in the darkness, hoping that his tabby friend hadn't got into any trouble.

2
Noble Creatures

Herbert was at that very moment sitting in his office at MI5 headquarters, which was located under a sculpture of Peter Pan in the middle of Hyde Park. The office was a mess of reports that needed reading, writing or filing, books that were left half open or firmly shut. The earthy brown walls were covered with shelves, overburdened with bits of evidence and various medals and cups, awards and pictures.

In front of him sat a thick file and a keen junior agent. "Thank you for the report. Tell me, does Kitty have any idea at all?" he asked, putting his large fluffy feet on the desk and flexing them next to his breakfast of a half-eaten iced bun and a cold cup of tea.

"Not sure, sir," said Chloe, the young field mouse. "We've several of our best Mice Intelligence agents watching Kitty. The Magpie Police spotted her in the vicinity of the Royal Stables, sir. I believe that she was visiting her Aunt Matilda. All reports lead me to believe that the palace cat has yet to learn the whereabouts of the ancient cat Queen Ebony. We are monitoring the situation and I'll keep you updated as to developments."

Herbert was pleased with the report. Twitching his whiskers, he stroked the front of his green cardigan, which felt a little tighter today. His brown eyes spied the half-eaten bun which was calling to him. He was going to have to lay off iced buns for a while. Forcing his gaze away, he found himself looking at a newspaper with a picture of Lupo at Horse Guards Parade, watching the Changing of the Guard with the Duke. The royal spaniel had learnt a lot about the incredibly hard-working horses of the Queen's Household Cavalry.

Herbert took off his horn-rimmed spectacles and rubbed them clean with a brilliant red hanky taken from the right hand pocket of his snug woolly cardigan. "And Vulcan, what is *he* up to?" His left ear twitched at the thought of the Queen's dorgi. He felt a twinge of sadness, and sighed. He had tried to train Vulcan but all his best efforts had been worthless. Vulcan was trouble – always had been. Lately, he seemed to be getting himself into all sorts of mischief. The dorgi was, in his opinion, not to be trusted.

"Sir, Vulcan seems to be very interested in Queen Victoria," said Chloe. "Curiously, he is spending a great deal of time cornering older palace mice, asking them about the Victorian royal pets and the history of Buckingham Palace. I looked into it, to try and get to the bottom of what he might be plotting. The only thing I found was that Queen Victoria surrounded herself with dogs. She had many different varieties – it looks to me like they were her guardians. But cats, sir . . . ?"

"Let me guess. You went looking for royal cats but found none? No one has ever seen a cat at Buckingham Palace. Most interesting indeed."

In response to the Head of MI5, the junior mouse agent shook her head.

"Fortunately when I was a younger agent I spent some time looking into Victorian pets and although I found no hard evidence, I think that the reason Buckingham Palace has no cats is because Queen Victoria was terrified of them!" said Herbert, blowing a big raspberry in the direction of the sumptuous iced bun.

The junior agent handed him her file. "This is everything, sir."

Herbert flicked open the cover. On the first page was a large picture of Queen Victoria. He muttered to himself, "*Noble By Name; By Nature Noble Too.*"

"Sorry, sir, did you say something?"

Clearing his throat, Herbert replied, "No, nothing of relevance yet, but it might be something later." He added to himself in a whisper: "Should we see any strange developments." Then he pulled on his long white whiskers and spoke up once again. "The key time, of course, shall be the eclipse. Better get everyone ready – just in case. In the meantime, put an extra agent on Burmese and Matilda. Kitty went to them for answers. Of that I am sure."

His tiny paw danced over the tempting treat. Instead, he picked up the tiny cup and saucer. His tea was cold enough for his liking. He sipped it slowly, reading the agents' notes. Thankfully, Ebony had not been found, neither by his agents nor any of the royal dogs. Buckingham Palace was safe from the curse. His stomach gurgled. Even his tummy knew trouble was heading towards the famous London palace.

"Just to be extra careful, let's dispatch a team to the palace to ask Holly to keep her eyes open for Kitty. She knows Kitty well enough to stop her from prowling into any trouble. My bigger concern is Lupo. He'll already be wondering why the palace cat is acting so mysteriously. The answers are, of course, all to be found at Buckingham Palace. He's smart enough to work this out for himself and when he does he will head straight to Holly for help."

When Lupo wandered through the main palace kitchens next morning, he saw that Kitty was still not back. Normally around this time she could be found circling the breakfast chef's legs, asking for scrambled eggs and warm milk. Her bowl sat untouched in the corner, where several mice were making the most of the free meal.

He tried finding her in the office that belonged to the palace dressmaker. Kitty liked to sit and watch her alter a dress or two for the Duchess or mend worn shoes for the Duke or George's uncle. Lupo's soft brown eyes examined the chair. No new cat hair. Quietly padding around the office, and sniffing, he could find no trace of her – but he did find the smallest and yet loudest mouse in Kensington Palace.

She was very handy so everyone referred to her as "Bobs", even though her real name was Annabel. Bobs was putting some fresh laces into the Duke's smart shoes. The old laces were going to be put to use in her latest invention, "shoes for mice".

"Morning, Bobs, have you seen Kitty or Herbert today?" Lupo asked.

"Morning, Lupo! No, but I'm heading straight over to MI5 – they want to investigate my latest invention. I don't think they like the idea of us mice wearing shoes," she said, looking a little forlorn. "Are we still meeting in the attic? My sources tell me that there are quite a few palace animals planning on watching the ghosts scare off all the visitors during the eclipse."

Lupo nodded, unsurprised that Bobs was so well informed. She seemed to know just about everyone.

"Great!" she said, leaping in the air. "I'll be sure to get a message to Herbert that you are looking for him! Bye – see you later!" She dived beneath a floorboard just as the dressmaker walked in.

"Morning, Lupo," said the dressmaker, making herself comfortable at her sewing machine. As she put her cup of steaming hot coffee down next to the shoes, she stopped, her mouth dropping open in astonishment. She had only left the room for a moment but had returned to find all her work had been done! The Duke's shoes looked smart with their brand-new laces. Lupo smiled at her reaction. The palace mice never failed to deliver a few good surprises!

Lupo made his way back into the apartment, stopping to pick up the small bundle of post marked "Private" for the Duke and Duchess. The pack of letters was heavier since the arrival of the new baby. There were lots of cards and wellwishers' letters amongst the usual children's party invitations. Normally he would drop them at the Duchess's feet but since she was too busy with the baby these days he delivered them to the Duke instead. The Duke, in turn, thanked him for his service and patted him on the head. "More cards, darling!" he said to the Duchess as he thumbed the pile.

Nanny grumbled loudly. Lupo could sense she was not in a good mood.

Prince George was bouncing around in his high chair, waving his wombat at the baby. George then thrust it in Lupo's face *booing* and *gooing*. "Goggles, look, Lupo! Wombat's wearing goggles!"

Lupo grinned broadly, licking his lips and waving his paw in the air. "I can't wait for the eclipse. It's going to be really scary! Whoo-hooo."

The Duchess comforted her sleeping baby. At the same time, she put George's egg and soldiers on a plate. George wailed with delight at the sight. The Duchess called for quiet and the Duke took the opportunity to take a big bite of his wife's marmalade on toast.

"That cat!" muttered Nanny as she bundled her way through to the laundry room.

It seemed that Kitty *had* been back and had left mucky paw prints all over Prince George's clean clothes. Nanny dumped the basket in front of the washing machine and then, muttering to herself some more, headed back to the nursery.

Lupo went to investigate the basket. He sniffed the pile. He picked up that Kitty had spent the night on the palace laundry. This was the first oddity. She had been around long enough to know that she would be in trouble for sleeping on clean clothes. The second thing was the pong of horse poo. Not common horses, either. Lupo was 98% confident that he could smell the royal stables, as they had a distinct heady mixture of boot polish and fresh hay mixed in with lime shampoo.

As the family sat down to breakfast, Lupo lay between the Duchess's pink slippers and the Duke's sheepskin-wearing feet, thinking. Kitty had gone to the stables to meet her Aunt Matilda, an old grey cat that lingered around the Queen's old horse, Burmese. Matilda was less than friendly and obviously didn't like royal dogs or young royals because she would disappear whenever Lupo and the buggy appeared.

Lupo was so distracted he nearly missed his own breakfast. Prince George had dropped a dippy egg under the table. Before anyone could stop him, Lupo licked the bright orange yolk out of the soft egg. Luckily, the Duchess was too busy yawning to notice him smacking his lips together with delight as the egg coated his short black nose.

As he finished his breakfast, he nuzzled George's chubby leg which thumped against the leg of the royal blue high chair. "I need your help, George. Kitty's still not back and I think she was at the stables. We need to go there to see the big horse Burmese." Prince George smiled cheekily and winked back at his dog. The Duchess sleepily reached out to George's half-eaten breakfast and picked up a lonely soldier of warm buttery toast.

"CLIP, CLOP, CLIP, CLOP!" sang George loudly, much to the whole table's excitement.

The Duke stood up and rushed over to his son's side. "Amazing, George, amazing! Did you hear that, darling? He definitely said 'Clip clop'! Horses, that's right, George – my clever little boy!"

"Horses?" said Duchess, looking mildly confused.

Nanny returned to the kitchen. "Oh yes! Horses!" she said, gently taking the sleeping baby from the tired Duchess. The baby cooed in her arms, ready for a nappy change. "Prince George likes visiting the horses. I take him to the stables sometimes because he likes to tickle the big one's nose. Maybe I'll take Lupo and Prince George this morning before Her Majesty's birthday at Buckingham Palace. Yes, we'll go to the horses, hey, Georgie?"

Lupo wasted no time and trotted off to the back

door to get his lead and collar. When he returned he sat waiting next to the buggy. Winking back at George, he said, "Nice one buddy. Thanks."

Prince George clapped, *burbling* joyfully. "Clip clop, clip, clop."

3
Burmese and Matilda

Matilda the grey cat rolled on to her side in the corner of the stable where she slept. She didn't mind having to share her home with the royal horse, Burmese. Sure, she was big and a bit smelly, and at times she acted like a gigantic oaf, but they were good stable companions.

Matilda groaned loudly as a mouse dived in and out of the soft hay. Burmese didn't mind the mice. In fact, she felt quite protective of the hard-working creatures. They would ferret around the stables, cleaning up misplaced straw and rescuing bits of tack that had been put away incorrectly. They helped, unlike the rats. None of the horses in the royal stables could stand the really fat rats. They roamed around late at night, stealing precious carrots

37

and apples from the stable stores.

Burmese thought it was a good thing having Matilda around, because the rats ran when they saw her. She barely had to lift a paw: one flick of her tail and the nasty, dirty beasts were racing down the cobbled yard to the nearest sewer. Burmese could understand why the rats liked coming to the royal stables – it was the best of the best – but in her old age she so disliked being disturbed by anything that irritated her: flies in the summer, rats in the winter.

In turn, Burmese had been there when Matilda had had her very last litter. The royal horse watched over all the litters over the years, like an overgrown babysitter. One hundred and seven kittens in total, all of them born in the corner of her humble palace stable. She would let the tiny little things sit on her back or try and grab and play with her long tail as it swished back and forth. When she slept she would often wake up to find them all tangled up in her mane. But those fun days with Matilda's kittens passed all too quickly. The furry little rascals would grow up and leave when their time came. The hardest thing was saying goodbye as they trooped off to their new homes around London. "Bye! Goodbye, Burmese!" they said as they waved.

Burmese hadn't always been a kitten-sitter. A long time ago she was a champion, and was fussed over day and night. People from all over the world would come to just get a glimpse of the Royal Stable's superstar. Pictures of her carrying the Queen during the Trooping of the Colour hung around the stables. Now she enjoyed her retirement with Matilda, resting until the time came for her to go to the stables in the sky.

The Queen still came to visit. She insisted on saying goodnight to all her horses whenever she was at Buckingham Palace. Wearing a fine silk scarf around her grey head, she would rub all the horses' noses and tickle their ears. But only Burmese would get fed a polo mint or a fat carrot. "Goodnight, old friend," she would whisper into Burmese's ear.

"Watch it, you great big brute!" said Matilda, disturbing Burmese's thoughts as the horse settled down and made herself more comfortable.

"Oh, that feels better," Burmese said. "Been on my feet all day. Come on, Matilda, tell me what's been happening. Was that Kitty I saw with you last night?"

Matilda picked up one of her paws and inspected the state of her claws. "Yes, it was Kitty – the high and mighty palace cat! She wants to talk to me. Apparently it's urgent and couldn't wait – she had to disturb my night's sleep. Humph."

Burmese found a nice bit of straw to chew on. "How is she? Haven't seen that little one since—"

"Since she took a ride on Milky's float to Kensington Palace!" said Matilda, annoyed that Burmese had forgotten Kitty's treachery. "She never came for *me*. I'm stuck here in this stinky stable and *she* is living the high life, salmon for breakfast, lunch and dinner, I'll bet!"

"Probably," said Burmese. "I bet she can have as many carrots as she likes." She imagined an enormous pile of the very best sweet orange vegetables.

"Is that all you think about? Carrots?" demanded Matilda. "Some of us have more important things on our minds!"

"Why would you want to think about anything other than carrots?" asked Burmese, confused.

At that moment, several younger horses neighed

in the next-door stables as the stable boys and girls began pouring buckets of oats into feeders. Burmese got to her feet.

"Something's up," said Matilda. "I can feel it in my tummy. Now who's coming and making all that noise?"

Just then, Prince George jumped up and down in his buggy as a young horse bent to sniff the heir to the throne's mop of blond hair. "Lupo! Horsey!"

Lupo was too busy sniffing the cobbles. He could smell the grey cat but wasn't able to pick up Kitty's scent, thanks to a new delivery of hay that was overpowering his strongest sense.

"What a fine young man," warbled an old horse who had once belonged to a general, as the buggy rolled past his stable. "Best hoof forward, everyone, the Prince has come to inspect us!"

One by one, the horses popped their heads over the stable doors to welcome the little Prince.

"Good morning, sir," said Lupo politely. "Thank you for welcoming us into your home. Prince George really enjoys coming to see you all here."

"Our pleasure, Lupo. It is an honour to have you here," said the finest of the royal service horses.

Commanding his officers to attention, he angled his long neck towards the adjacent stable. "CAPTAIN! STAND TO! ROYAL DOG PRESENT!"

Lupo bowed his head, thanking the royal horses. Up ahead he could see Burmese smiling down at the royal visitors. When at last the buggy arrived at her stables she neighed as loudly as she could. "Lupo, my friend! How have you been? Hasn't Prince George grown? How's the baby? Duchess OK?"

Lupo smiled a toothy grin at the old horse. Nanny took George to investigate the new foals.

"Thank you, Burmese. Yes, we are all doing very well at Kensington Palace. I was hoping I might get a chance to talk to you. You see . . ." started Lupo, before being rudely interrupted.

"Where else would Burmese be?!" chided Matilda, suddenly appearing over the top of the stable door.

"Hello, I'm Lupo," he began, as Matilda turned to walk away, uninterested in the royal visitors. "And you are . . . ?"

"Matilda! That's my name, don't wear it out!" said the grey cat.

Burmese stuck her nose out, forcing the old cat to

the side of the door. "Excuse my friend. She is old and tired and extremely RUDE!"

"WATCH IT, you nearly pushed me out!" responded Matilda.

"Sorry, Matilda has no manners," Burmese went on. "She won't even acknowledge the Queen. Something about cats not being welcome in the royal palaces or some such. How can we be of assistance?"

"I am looking for Kitty," explained Lupo. "I think she may have been here recently. She mentioned that she was coming to see you. She told me that she wanted to talk to you about Ebony."

But before he could finish, Matilda peered into his brown eyes for answers. "How do you know about Ebony?" she demanded.

"That's just it. I don't," Lupo tried. "I was hoping . . ."

"No, you don't want to know about such things. You're a dog and dogs have no business in cat matters. *Especially* ROYAL DOGS," meowed Matilda angrily.

Burmese reached over, grabbed the moody grey cat by the scruff of her neck and carefully plopped her down into her bed. "Now, you stay there and behave yourself. If you can't play nicely you'll have to

go to bed!" She turned around and walked to the stable door, then bent low to Lupo's ear so as not to stir Matilda further. The horse whispered loudly: "Kitty *was* here last night. I overheard them. Kitty said they needed to talk about the Prince's journals – you know, the ones in the paper that were found at Buckingham Palace?"

"Yes, I know. Did they say anything about Ebony?"

"Matilda didn't seem that bothered about them. She said that the chances of anyone finding the lost ancient cat were slim to none. She told Kitty to relax and to meet her in the City of Creatures – some place called the Katz Bar, I think?"

The buggy wheels were covered in hay when they returned. Burmese tried to lick Nanny, who smiled awkwardly at the Queen's horse's affections.

Nanny said, "Time to go. It's a big day for you, Georgie! Off to Buckingham Palace for the Queen's birthday! Cake, Georgie, yay!"

Lupo thanked Burmese and said goodbye to the rest of the stable horses. Nanny sneezed loudly as she wheeled the buggy into the warm morning sunshine.

* * *

One of the palace mice had left Lupo an MI5 memo of the day's schedule, which he had found in his unused bed in the kitchen. As his royal dog training demanded, he quickly memorised it, and then destroyed it:

(Royal baby to Grandparents for the day.)
Rest of family to attend following events:-
Queen's Birthday Ceremony at Westminster Abbey
Royal Family Birthday Lunch at Buckingham Palace Banqueting Hall
OFFICIAL BIRTHDAY PORTRAIT in the Throne Room
Viewing of the Eclipse
Presents for the Queen – in the living room with special birthday cake
Buckingham Palace Balcony Wave
Dinner at Buckingham Palace with President of the United States and All Foreign Ambassadors
Gala Concert (Very Important People Only) Buckingham Palace

***

Lupo found the young Prince crying in the Nursery. George didn't like being fussed over but because today was his great grandmother's birthday, he was being fussed over a lot. New clothes were being put on him following a mid-morning bath.

The Duke was attempting to help Nanny. "Now, George, calm down. Birthdays are special! We are all going to Buckingham Palace to a party and to watch the eclipse. Won't that be good? There is even a very special carrot cake. I know you love cake!"

But George had lost his wombat and tears rolled heavily down his plump pink cheeks. He *gurgled* to Lupo, "Wombat?"

Lupo shook his coat and winked at the sad little Prince. "I'll find it."

He traced the wombat's scent to the Duke and Duchess's room. It was lying on the side of the bed, looking quite unloved. Lupo jumped on to the covers, picked the toy up and held it gently in his mouth.

The Duchess was in her private dressing room, sitting in front of a mirror, adjusting a small cream hat with

47

a scary wiggly pointy thing sticking out the top of it. She patted Lupo on the head as he walked out. "Thank you, Lupo. George just can't be without that toy for a second." Her big blue sapphire ring shimmered on her slim finger. "We'll be out until very late today. That means you won't have George to keep you company. If Kitty ever returns you can hang out with her," she said. "Just don't go getting yourself into any trouble."

Lupo sat at the back door as he watched his family being escorted through the courtyard of the palace and into a fleet of security cars. George was wearing a smart blue outfit, which he had already managed to make dirty (much to Nanny's annoyance). He looked over his daddy's shoulder and waved to Lupo as he was carried towards the car.

Loyally, Lupo stood perfectly still, on guard. He was George's guardian. But his black feathery paws shook, because he didn't like being separated from the young Prince. The only good thing was that it gave him a chance to find out a bit more about Ebony and the curse that had Kitty on the run. He needed to see the journals for himself, which meant he would have to go to Buckingham Palace. The problem with this was that as much as he yearned to have an adventure, today was not the day to be solving cursed mysteries around that royal residence!

4
City of Creatures

The guardian of the tunnel was a particularly spindly character. She was a very large common black spider, who was used to being chased out of the bath tub by a screaming Duchess and being swept out into the garden by a helpful palace servant. But having a fully-grown cocker spaniel invading her home was quite another thing. It had been fine having him come and visit them when he had been a fluffy puppy but now that he was "a big hairy thing with those scary long legs" she quite disapproved of her growing family getting overjoyed at his arrival and winding themselves all up about him.

"Lupo, I haven't seen you here in a while," she said, hoping that he wasn't about to start using this entrance regularly.

"Lupo!" cheered hundreds of baby spiders as he bent and wiggled to get under the long bottom shelf which was laden with unloved tins of fruit and vegetables.

"Hi there, everyone!" he said, a little sheepishly. He was fully aware that he was crushing his way through a very tidy-looking web. "It's a pleasure to see you – Mrs Spider, you are looking very well. Have you lost weight?"

"Lupo, you flatter me, but no! I am pleased to tell you that I am pregnant again, actually. It seems the great and good have blessed us with more little spiders. Mind out, Harold, Lupo is coming through," she yelled to her husband, who was busy wrapping a bluebottle up for the family's eclipse picnic.

"Now!" cried a team of teenage spiders as they abseiled on silk from the top shelf down to investigate the commotion. At first, they were disappointed to find that it was only Lupo, but then they busied themselves hooking on to his dark fur. They all spoke at once: "Take us with you, Lupo! Mum won't let us go along the Red route until we are older. What's it like at Buckingham Palace?"

Lupo obliged. "Your mum is right – it's no place

for young spiders."

The spider grouped the silk threads of her teens together, causing them all to bunch up uncomfortably. "Leave Lupo alone. Off to the top shelf the lot of you."

At that, their tiny faces and blinking eyes fell downcast. The group crept off, leaving Lupo alone with their mother at the entrance to the Red route.

The royal passageways were clearly mapped and no matter which route you travelled along you knew that you would end up at a royal residence. They were safe, clean and relatively comfortable with limited dangers, so that royal animals could stroll along them 24/7.

The kickboard was loose enough for a small creature to climb through. Lupo could feel a strong draught. The spider inched her way forward, offering to open the way for the royal dog. Lupo thanked the spider and headed in. It was his first trip alone without the help of his friends.

Lupo took a sharp intake of breath at the sight of all the royal animal portraits adorning the walls. Eos, the greyhound that had tided up the secret animal passages, stood to attention in his large gold frame. Prince Albert's beloved pet had changed the way the palace animals lived, communicated and travelled. Without these passages the royal animals would have been trapped within their homes, and unable to explore the wonders of the world that other animals took for granted. Lupo bowed respectfully as he passed the picture.

Every now and then he looked up to see where he was. As he reached Rotten Row – the sandy bridleway that runs through the far end of Hyde Park – he saw that the next stop on the route was Hyde Park Corner, marked by a hand-painted picture of the roundabout's enormous sculpture of the angel and her horses. When he turned left, he knew he was below Constitutional Hill: he could see the end of the line. A sharp right ahead would take him all the way to the entrance to England's most famous palace.

It had been a long time since Kitty had visited the City of Creatures which humans dared not visit. It was made up of hundreds of interconnecting tunnels that ran deep under London. Unlike the smart royal passageways the tunnels were not richly decorated or coloured.

Kitty was used to travelling down the Red route to Buckingham Palace, or across the Blue route to Windsor Castle. It had been a while since she had visited Hampton Court on the Yellow or braved the long cold route from London to Balmoral using the Green.

Down in the City of Creatures she found herself well and truly out of her comfort zone; lost and a little bit lonely. It was dark and damp, and very dangerous in parts. There were tunnels within the city where strange animals lived hidden amongst shabby homes made of rubbish. Man's trash was the City of Creatures' treasure. Animals and their bustling trading businesses thrived down here. Kitty marvelled at the sight of a busy marketplace where animals argued over their finds. As she walked on, she kept herself amused wondering what a human would make of the world beneath their feet. A Watcher bat raced past, reminding her that there was a system in place just in case a brave and terribly stupid human should attempt to find the city. Thanks to the Watcher bats, swallows and rats there was always someone waiting for the slightest sign of trouble from "them up-top".

As Kitty rounded a corner, a smell of putrid fish and waste filled her nostrils. She purred softly to calm her nerves. She recognized this part of the city. The tunnel was made up of hundreds of old limestone cobbles. Urban animals including cats, foxes, squirrels, rats and mice made their homes within it. Some had sumptuous allocated quarters, others had to put up with less habitable homes, squabbling over every bit of space amongst the soft stone tunnels. There were also the darker, less common creatures, like crocodiles, snakes and terrifying monsters. They kept to themselves, well hidden in the tunnels' dankness.

London cats gathered in large numbers at a place called the Katz Bar. It had been a long time since her last visit there. On rare occasions she liked to hear what was happening out in the real world – it was her way of checking in. But over the years she'd found that being in the City of Creatures made her feel uncomfortable and she longed to get back to her laundry basket within George's uncle's apartment.

Before she saw the bar, Kitty heard the cat calls bouncing restlessly off the rounded walls. When she arrived she could see several older cats outside its entrance playing with a dirty bit of wool and what looked like a petrified rat. They were clearly enjoying themselves as the rat attempted to escape the claws and loud cackles.

Matilda was nowhere in sight, so Kitty wandered in and asked a young cat behind the bar for a bottle of milk. All around, kittens and cats of all ages were seeking refuge from the humans above. The young cat delivered the milk meekly before serving a large group of old alley cats that were looking for food and shelter. Kitty reminded herself of how lucky she was living at Kensington Palace; she could have easily ended up lost, left behind or abandoned.

Matilda was late, which Kitty thought was quite rude. When she eventually arrived she lurched forwards and hugged the tabby, and her long, un-groomed white whiskers bristled the side of Kitty's face, tickling and irritating her. Kitty couldn't help but notice Matilda's saggy belly that hung as heavily now as it did when it sheltered the many litters she left all over London.

Matilda was in a bad mood. Some bicycle boy had run over her tail and it was stiff and crooked. She flopped on to the floor in front of Kitty, praying that the tabby would give her the sympathy she craved.

Kitty wasn't in the mood for her aunt's moaning, but Bertie's journals had unnerved her. She wanted to find out if her royal family was in danger. As much as Kitty hated to admit it, Matilda had her paw on the pulse of the city.

Kitty asked, "I need you to tell me about Bertie's journals and the ancient cat Queen Ebony."

"Is that it?" her aunt replied. "When you showed up last night you said it was urgent! I have been travelling all morning to get here. When you said it was about Ebony I thought you had found her! Let me understand – you woke me up in the middle of the night for some old books and a dusty old legend? Do you know how long it takes to get to sleep in those stables? *DO YOU?*"

Kitty licked her milk, ignoring

Matilda's questions. She had come for answers.

Matilda signalled the young cat to come over with more milk. "No, 'hello Auntie Matilda' just straight in for the kill! OF COURSE I've heard about those journals. I CAN READ the paper, you know. Who knows what humans will find out from them. Who cares?" cursed the tired grey cat, grabbing a half-drunk bottle of milk from a sleeping kitten.

Kitty stood and arched her back. "I need you to tell me the story about Ebony again. I can't remember all of it and now that the journals have been found there is a chance someone might find her and I can't risk my family being hurt by her curse."

"Family – by that I take it you are referring to that dog, Lupo, huh? I would hardly call that spaniel *family*! *I* am your family – or have you forgotten you're a *cat*? Just like Ebony. *We* are your family. Not some royal dog who pants after a Prince and a few posh mice. You think you are so high and mighty, Kitty, but you are not. You are just a plain old tabby that got lucky. It could have just as easily been me that got caught in the royal cream! Don't you forget it!"

"Please, auntie. If I thought I could ask anyone

else I would, but only cats know Ebony's story so I'm stuck with having to ask you. By the way, Lupo *is* family to me. He doesn't have a clue about any of this. Please, I need your help. Little Prince George means everything to him," said Kitty, increasingly annoyed with her aunt's attention-seeking attitude.

"All right, all right, I'll tell you. A nice bedtime story," offered Matilda.

"It can't wait until bedtime," Kitty cried. "Please, can we have a nice little chat about Ebony and I will take a look at that tail for you? It looks bad – you're going to have to start taking better care of yourself. Aren't you on your ninth life?"

Matilda lay flat on her side to let Kitty examine the scuffed tail. "I may very well be on my last life. Some days it feels like I am on my first and others I might as well be on my ninth. If only Ebony was around today. She would give me back my nine lives and I would be able to start all over again. Just a moment in her presence is all I need."

Purring, she melted against Kitty and closed her eyes, ready to tell Ebony's story.

"Ebony was so powerful," she began. "She could

grant all kinds of wishes. Some say she was a goddess. For sure, she was the kind of cat that is born once in a million generations. They say that the night she was born the sun disappeared in the middle of the day. An eclipse lasting a full hour spread across the ancient world. Animals retreated into their homes, praying that it was not the end. The human pharaoh was so frightened, he summoned all his priests to his inner sanctum and begged the gods to bring back the light. They didn't fail him. But that wasn't all they gave to the world, those pesky ancient gods. Black like the day she was born, Ebony arrived on the back of the largest crocodile that lived on the River Nile. Don't try that, Kitty – riding on the back of one of the crocodiles down here. I knew a cat who—"

"The story!" Kitty squeezed the end of Matilda's tail. "Get back to the story!"

"Ouch! Ebony was a cat that could change the world. Word travelled fast amongst all animals of her powers."

"What was her skill, Auntie? Why where all the animals so in awe of her?" demanded Kitty.

"Not a skill, but a gift from the gods themselves.

Our legend says that Ebony could get into the mind of any animal. She could whisper to your very soul! Kitty, not even you could resist her orders once she was in your mind! In there she could get you to do her darkest bidding. But me? No, she would never get in to *my* mind because I'm too wise and stubborn," purred Matilda.

"That's not possible. Animals can't speak through thought alone." Kitty stood and paced uncomfortably. Several cats poured into the Katz Bar and nodded in their direction. Kitty's eyes caught her aunt's. "But I remember you told me that she was half human, half cat?"

"No, in life she had the body of a human girl but the face and wisdom of a dark cat," Matilda explained. "The humans fell at her feet believing her to be superhuman. Crowds would gather to see her walking amongst the humans and animals alike. The Pharaoh was so scared he had failed the gods that he bowed low to Ebony, doing all that she asked. She did not miss her opportunity. She demanded that he free all the slaves and release all the animals. He was too scared to say no, and it was his undoing. Ebony was handed the Pharaoh's sceptre."

Kitty was lost in a vivid thought about Ebony's terrific reign. "What happened to her?" she finally questioned.

"It's unclear. All I know is that a dog was involved. A dog and some humans who felt that it wasn't right to be ruled by a cat. There was some kind of tussle for the throne and Ebony lost her human traits. She became a pure black cat with haunting green eyes. I think it's more than likely the Romans captured her. We know for definite that they destroyed every record of her existence. They smashed up her sculptures and buried her kingdom under the sands. Either way, Ebony's reign was at an end."

"A dog?" queried Kitty. "That's odd. I don't think I remember you saying anything about a dog before."

"Well, as I said, it really is all rumours now. I think the dog was some kind of a god. I suspect he delivered her to the underworld."

Kitty swallowed a pesky hairball that was stuck hard in her throat. "The curse, Matilda. Tell me about Ebony's curse."

Matilda sat like a sphinx, facing Kitty. "The curse of dreamless sleep will befall anyone who disturbs her. The curse is real. As *she* was. This much I know is true. We are living proof. You see, the night Ebony died she was hastily buried by her human priests. But at dawn the following day, the priests noticed she was missing. She had been taken by a group of cats who put her in a lavish tomb. As they moved her sarcophagus into place, apparently Ebony awoke – as if from a dream. She warned that she would return to the earth and seek her revenge against the humans. She would take back her kingdom and *cats would rule!* She said that she would rise again during a full eclipse and that she would have the power to command the sands of time by whipping up great big sandstorms! Ebony will put all the humans to sleep. She would start with Bertie's royal family, since it was he who disturbed her tomb. She will curse them all to a dark dreamless sleep! Those journals of his have all the answers. If the humans knew how to read them, they would see that the hieroglyphics served as a warning."

She paused before continuing. "Kitty, be in no doubt. Ebony will bring about the end of the human monachy and we – the descendants of her guardians – will receive a gift for our loyalty. Ebony gave us the gift of nine lives. She swore that one day we would have our day alongside her when she arose."

"But . . ." Kitty was struggling to take in everything she was being told.

"When the streets are empty and the houses and palaces are quiet, we can rule just as she did. It will finally be our time."

"Today there will be a full eclipse," Kitty reflected. "Does this mean that she could wake?"

"Kitty, you worry too much! So what if she did wake up? It would be good news! Cats would rule the world!"

"I *have* to find Lupo," Kitty cried. "Where is Ebony now, Matilda? Where?" The desperation was rising in her throat.

But the old grey cat was lost in her own excitement. "Can you imagine it, Kitty? The whole royal family falling asleep no matter what they were doing. What if the Queen was eating soup? SPLOSH! Or drinking hot tea? OUCH! Just one shake of Ebony's sacred rattle and every human from here to eternity would be asleep!"

Kitty was shocked. "Auntie! Snap out of it!"

Matilda laughed madly. "Oh, you silly cat! You have nothing to be afraid of. She remains only in the form of dusty sculptures in human museums. No one knows where she is. The only clue to where her tomb might be found is in Bertie's silly journals. Ebony is lost."

5
The King's Study

There was more than one way into Buckingham Palace, Lupo remembered as he found himself standing at a fork in the passageway. He knew he risked taking the wrong exit and ending up in completely the wrong part of the building.

Thankfully, Eos had drawn a map of all Buckingham Palace's secret entrances and exits, and this hung on the wall. Lupo sat down and studied it for a while.

The Commoners' Pantry looked like a very old entrance since it was very faded on the map. The King's Study's entrance was between a pair of bookcases. He thought: we don't have a King, only a Queen. Perhaps that's George's great-grandfather's study? He'd only ever met the Queen's husband once and he seemed like a very nice man. Lupo decided that appearing in his private study in the middle of the morning probably wouldn't be a good idea on any normal day, but today he was bound to be at Westminster Abbey with the rest of the family, leaving the King's Study unattended. Once he was in, he could try and find the journals before the family returned from the Abbey.

Time was slipping by, so he had to hurry.

Kitty was making her way out of the City of Creatures when she bumped into Herbert. It was no accident. Herbert had come looking for her. Three of his fastest agents had sent word back to HQ that Kitty had been in the Katz Bar meeting with Matilda.

Herbert had a soft spot for Kitty. She was a tabby who had been quite lost before she made it to Kensington Palace. A milk float had carried her all the way to the palace kitchen door. Half starved and in need of a good home, the staff had taken her in, fed and loved her. She'd revelled in her new surroundings, keeping an eye on everything. Some years later, Herbert had overheard a group of kittens from the stables talking about her in hallowed terms, such was the loyalty she commanded. There was little doubt that she was a powerful member of the cat community. She wasn't well loved by mice, but that didn't seem to bother her. She once told him, "Mice don't like cats, dogs don't like cats. We cats fit in were we can." It helped that she didn't like eating mice, of course.

Herbert admired her extensive royal knowledge, even though she had never been schooled. She had once said something very wise to Lupo, who was doing his best to disrupt a History lesson. "Queen Victoria's love of dogs did little to help the cat population, Lupo. People abandoned their cats in favour of Pekingese, spaniels, greyhounds and those dreadful snuffling pugs. Thousands of cats were forced underground into the City of Creatures. Thankfully, things changed over time and the balance was restored. But we still have those very same underground lodges for those less fortunate, mostly unloved cats."

Now Herbert played it cool. He was quick to explain to the surprised cat that he was heading to Buckingham Palace to check the arrangements for the Queen's birthday and the eclipse. He casually

dropped in the fact that he was going to inspect Bertie's journals.

"So that's why I'm here. What a pleasant surprise to see you! This isn't your usual stalking ground, is it?" said Herbert, nervously adjusting his spectacles.

The tabby was keen to get on herself, but pleased to see Herbert. Even though she found most mice an irritant, she was always happy to see the Head of Mice Intelligence Section 5. "Herbert, always a pleasure. No, not somewhere I tend to visit very regularly."

"Been doing anything interesting here in the City? Visiting anyone in particular?" he questioned carefully.

Kitty decided it was best not to involve Herbert. "No, no one special. Right . . . well, I'd best be heading back to Kensington. No doubt Lupo will be wondering where I am."

"Ahh, yes! Well, I'd best be off, too. Lots to do at Buckingham Palace before the eclipse."

Just as the mouse turned to leave, Kitty felt an urge to test his well-regarded knowledge of all things. "Hey, Herbert! I don't suppose you know where exactly in Buckingham Palace they found

Bertie's journals, do you?"

Herbert gulped hard. "Err . . . Human newspapers claim it was in that dusty trap-infested library," the mouse said cautiously. "But you can't believe everything you read in the papers. I have a sneaking suspicion they were somewhere much less obvious. You know, these funny things tend to show up in the most bizarre places. I wouldn't be surprised if my mice hand me a report saying that they were found under a dusty old sofa or some such!" He turned his back and waved goodbye, both at the same time.

Kitty couldn't put her paw on it but she could tell he wasn't telling her something. She leapt high in the air and landed smack in front of the terrified mouse.

"Mind, Kitty! You nearly landed on my head!" blurted Herbert.

"What is it that you aren't telling me, my soft little friend?" She curled her sandpaper tongue inside her mouth.

Herbert held his ground. "Kitty, if there *was* something, you know that as Head of MI5 I am not at liberty to discuss it. You will have to wait, like everyone else, until we have conducted a full investigation."

"Of course. What is it that you are investigating?" Kitty asked cleverly.

"Clearly, you are not going to let this go." He couldn't pretend any longer. "Look, Kitty, I know you have been trying to find out the whereabouts of Queen Ebony. You must stop." He paused, then revealed: "I am concerned that Queen Ebony was quite powerful in her day and I wouldn't want her to be disturbed. Eternal rest is meant to be eternal – I've never quite understood why humans had to dig everyone up and disturb those poor pharaohs . . ."

He stopped when he saw Kitty's green eyes flash with recognition. "How did you know I was worried about Ebony?" she asked.

"Why, of course, my dear, I am the Head of MI5. It is my job to know everything!" answered Herbert proudly. Just then, Kitty started to count. "What are you doing?" demanded Herbert.

"You are going to need my help. I'm counting the number of times I have seen something Egyptian in any of the palaces," offered Kitty.

Herbert was concerned. "Now Kitty, this is not something you need to bother yourself with. Lupo and the family . . ."

"Lupo and the family are the reason why I *am concerning* myself." Kitty arched her back, annoyed that Herbert thought he could tell her what to do.

"I assure you, my best mice are working on it as we speak," said Herbert.

"Then you won't mind if I tag along," Kitty replied. "Many paws make quick work!"

"Oh!" said Herbert, seeing that he wasn't going to stop her from getting her own way. "Well, OK, if you insist."

"You think Ebony is at Buckingham Palace – *that's* why you are going there, isn't it?"

"I'm not sure but, yes, I think it is highly probable that she is somewhere within the Palace. Unfortunately my mice are having a bit of trouble finding her."

Lupo stood in the middle of the King's Study. A ticking grandfather clock and some very tall bookshelves surrounded a grand English fireplace. There was a desk at one end of the room. Behind it was a thick mulberry-coloured leather chair. He made sure that the entrance door between the bookcases was firmly shut before sniffing the air to see if he could pick up Holly's smell. He detected

73

musky cologne – but not Holly. She smelt of freshly cut grass and roses on a summer's day.

There was a soft breeze coming from one of the double bay windows behind the leather chair. Lupo went to the window and stood on his hind legs to look out over the gardens behind the palace. From his perch he could see all the way to the edge of the lake where he and Holly liked to sit and talk. There was no sign of her or any of the other royal dogs in the garden.

At that moment, he heard a noise behind him. Turning his head, still standing on his hind legs, he saw that there was a large sheet of blue paper on the desk. Its edges were being tickled by the breeze coming in from the window. It fluttered, enticing him to take a peep.

Looking around, he listened to see if anyone was coming, and sensed that the coast was clear. So in one swift move he jumped into the plump leather chair. Resting both his front paws on the desk, he was able to steady himself enough to see the pages.

The large blue sheet showed a rubbing. It looked like a series of drawings had been traced on to the paper. The little pictures were of animals. Lupo

thought that it was like old Egyptian hieroglyphics – but somehow different. The pictures were more detailed and the animals in the thin drawings appeared to be dancing. As he looked on, the animals danced more and more frantically.

"What does it mean?" he said out loud.

It was clear to him that George's great-grandfather had also been trying to work out what the pictures meant. Pencil notes in the corners of the pages said:

Hawk? Or Parrot? – Giraffe? Or Horse?
Elephant that dances – Charging with strength?

Lupo wondered what the Queen's husband was studying. He wondered if the strange pictures of ancient animals dancing had anything to do with the unexpected appearance of Bertie's journals.

Just as he jumped down from the desk he momentarily looked up and saw that the desk had a small bronze token pinned underneath it. It read:

Dear Bertie,

Safe travels to the ancient world.

Write as often as you can.

VR

VR – Victoria Regina! Queen Victoria's signature. Lupo had seen those letters on more than one occasion in Kensington Palace.

"So this was Bertie's desk!" he said triumphantly.

Lupo sniffed it for more clues. It appeared to be like any other wooden desk, sturdy and strong. There were three drawers on the front left-hand side and – he counted "One, two, three . . . four!" – on the right-hand side. That's odd, he thought. Why would there be three on one side and four on the other?

He pulled open the fourth drawer on the right. It was not as deep as the others, and inside he was shocked to find a statue of a human with the head and face of a cat. "The Egyptian cat," Lupo whispered. Reaching into the drawer, he pulled the statue out. It was heavy. He rubbed it with his paw and the browning statue started to glint, revealing its hidden secrets.

The small figure was covered in the same strange drawings that were on the desk. At the base of the statue was the word:

EBONY

Lupo's right ear twitched. Someone was coming towards the door of the King's study. Footsteps sounded in the corridor – heavy footwear. It *had* to be a human. Quickly, he replaced the statue and slid the drawer closed. Then he hid himself under the desk and waited to see who was coming. There were benefits to being a dark-coloured dog.

The doorknob turned and in walked George's great-grandfather. He was very tall in the flesh. Lupo waited until the Queen's husband had walked around the desk before slipping out the other side, thereby avoiding being trodden on. Lupo stood as still as he could against the side of the desk and waited.

"Now, where was I . . ." mumbled the wise man. "Ah yes, here we are. Flapping bird . . . looks like a heron."

The telephone shrilled loudly on the desk rang.

"Yes?" he answered. "What is it? . . . Yes dear,

right-oh. Yes . . . No, I'm looking at that rubbing from Bertie's . . . No, dear, I haven't managed to work it out. Yes dear, very strange stuff. When's lunch? Right-oh! Be leaving any minute . . . No, I won't be late." He finished the telephone call and went back to his drawings briefly before there was a knock at the study door. "YES, come in!"

The Queen's eldest grandchildren walked in. "Come on, Grandpapa – it's lunchtime!" Behind them were Holly and Willow. Both corgis failed to notice Lupo hiding behind an old worn-out armchair covered in fading red roses.

As the old Duke stood up to leave he stooped over the pictures and said, "Just wish I could work out what it all meant. It's the strangest thing . . . got me stumped . . . Right-oh lunch, then . . . children, help your grandpapa over to that Banqueting Hall. You know how much Grandma hates me being late for these formal things."

Lupo watched as everyone made their way out of the study. He noticed that Holly was last to leave. "PSSSSSTTTTT . . . HOLLY!" he whispered loudly.

Holly was delighted to see her friend in the corner

79

of the room. "Lupo! What are *you* doing here?"

"I need your help. I'll explain everything – have you seen Bertie's journals?" Lupo's heart was beating that bit louder now that he was faced with the beautiful corgi.

"Hang on!" she said. "Please don't tell me you're involved in that ancient cat stuff too? The whole palace has been talking about it all week!"

"They have?" Lupo was surprised.

Holly was amused at the look on Lupo's handsome face. "Of course. Ever since the Queen's husband found the journals in that old desk everyone has been trying to work out what it all means."

"I think it means trouble." Lupo looked back over to the desk. He wondered if it contained any other items of curiosity.

Holly saw how important it was to Lupo. "If it helps, I can tell you that Ebony was a pharaoh. Pretty cool, huh? Who would have thought? A cat ruling humans – it's bizarre. You couldn't imagine it happening today. Mind you, it has everyone talking. You should hear the maids gossiping about the hidden room. Quite funny, really."

Lupo's ears pricked up. "A pharaoh? How do you

know that? Was it in the journals?"

Holly explained, "Not quite. Let's just say I was in the right place at the right time. When I was a pup I got lost once and ended up in the hay in the royal stables. I was lonely and pretty scared. I overheard a cat telling her kittens a bedtime story about some awful cat called Ebony who once ruled over Egypt as a pharaoh. Nasty business, if you ask me. Anyway, she was some kind of goddess, half human, half cat, until she was taken to the underworld by a dog."

"I don't suppose this cat mentioned anything about a curse?" asked Lupo.

"No, I think I would have remembered that," answered Holly.

No wonder Kitty was scared, thought Lupo. "Kitty overheard the Duke telling George and me about the journals. She seemed to be quite disturbed about a curse. Holly, you don't think Ebony is here in Buckingham Palace, in this hidden room the maids are gossiping about?"

"I've been trying to piece things together myself," said Holly. "I found out that Queen Victoria wrote to Bertie saying that she was devastated to hear that he had wasted such an important opportunity

81

to promote Britain *gathering trinkets*. In her diary, the palace housekeeper at the time says that Victoria was so scared of the boxes Bertie sent back from Egpyt that she had the entire contents locked up in a hidden room here at Buckingham Palace. So I believe that it's very possible that Ebony is still lost here."

"Let me guess – no one knows which room?" offered Lupo.

"Exactly! It's quite the mystery. Not sure the Queen approves, though. This is her birthday week and what with that and the eclipse excitement, she's not exactly thrilled that her husband is too tired to attend all the functions. Poor Candy and Monty have been following him every night. He's hunting for that room. Housekeepers found him fast asleep in the corner of a broom cupboard the other morning." Holly went very quiet when she heard a dog's paws pausing outside the study. She looked at the door and said in a low whisper, "It's Vulcan. He's up to no good. I can feel it."

Lupo had to resist the urge to growl. He murmured, "If you think Vulcan's up to something, he probably is. But why the Queen's dorgi would be interested in finding an old cat is beyond me. Unless, of course, he's after something else." Holly smiled at him. He tried not to get distracted by her pretty face. Blushing, he asked, "Holly, what else did the housekeeper's diary say?"

Now Vulcan's paws could be heard walking back down the corridor, away from the room.

"Why are you so interested? There was nothing other than the list of what was in the packing boxes Bertie had sent over from Cairo."

Lupo scratched his belly and sat down on an old hand-woven rug. "Holly, Kitty knows something about this cat Queen Ebony and *I* want to know what she's hiding from me. I have a feeling in my belly that something bad is about to happen here. The other night we talked about the eclipse and a curse. I am beginning to think the two are connected. I think we have to find that hidden room before the eclipse."

"OK, I'll help but what do you think is going to happen, Lupo?" asked Holly.

"I don't know exactly," said Lupo. "Maybe nothing."

Holly bowed her head. "Well, if you have a bad

feeling that's enough for me," she said. "I'll help you but first I just need to check I won't be missed. The family is in the Banqueting Hall. Lunch is being served and I'll need to see that Vulcan is occupied. The last thing we need is to have him following us."

6

A Hidden Room

Her Majesty the Queen was standing in front of her family as the Master of Ceremonies announced the national anthem. Everyone in the hall stood to sing – unaware that Prince George was clapping because he could see Lupo and Holly poking their heads around the door.

Lupo looked about him, checking every now and then that no one was walking down the vast hallway. He could see Monty, Willow and Candy under the table in the long elegant room. But he couldn't see the dog he didn't want to bump into . . . Vulcan. If Vulcan knew Lupo was in Buckingham Palace uninvited, he would find a way to have him removed.

As the music began, Holly snuck in. Lupo smiled as she dived under the extended dining table. Holly was sniffing the carpet, hoping to pick up Vulcan's scent. No one seemed to notice her ferreting around. Lupo heard a clink and then a clank. He turned and looked up to the ceiling and immediately spotted two palace mice swinging on a chandelier. They seemed to be in a big hurry. He did his best to keep up with them as they leapt from one chandelier to the next, jumping on the expensive crystals.

"Hurry, Kaye! Hurry! I want to show it to you before the eclipse!" said one of the mice.

"Charlotte, where did you say you found it?" asked the other.

"I just found it! I'm telling you, it's a perfect home. It can be all ours!" answered Charlotte. Her little brown body flew through the air like a rocket.

"No one just *finds* a hidden room, Charlotte!" said Kaye, taking a huge flying leap through the air and landing on a bust of Prince Albert.

"Shhhhhuuuuussshhhhh! We don't want everyone knowing – it's our secret!" said Charlotte, as she leapt on to the floor, waiting for her friend to catch up.

"Charlotte, stop rocketing around. I'm struggling to keep up!"

Lupo tried to follow but the mice dived into the tiniest hole behind a table leg. Still determined, he sniffed the air, trying to track them. It was no good: they had squeezed into the smallest of spaces and were no doubt running between the walls, so he didn't get the chance to ask about the mysterious hidden room. But heading back to the door of the Banqueting Hall, he convinced himself that the chances of a lost room and a hidden room being one and the same was highly likely.

Little did he know that something very old and very dark was beginning to stir in the oldest part of Buckingham Palace – and the tiny mice were headed right for it.

Vulcan smelt something fishy going on. His whiskers twitched at the sight of Holly scurrying around beneath the table – and Lupo sticking his head around the door to the Hall. Whenever he felt threatened, the hair on Vulcan's back stood straight up. Lupo's presence in the palace enraged him. "If he thinks he can roam around like he owns the place, he's wrong! That dog doesn't belong here."

Hopping down from the Queen's granddaughter's lap Vulcan sauntered up to Candy and asked pointedly, "What's *he* doing here?"

Candy was nibbling politely on a plastic bone one of the princes had given her to chew. The bright pink bone the Duchess had given Vulcan remained untouched.

The Queen's dog stopped chewing. "Vulcan, you have tried every trick in the book to get rid of him. Don't think I didn't notice that stunt you pulled when the President of the United States came to visit. Honestly, Vulcan, stealing the President's hamburger and dumping it next to Lupo was just plain immature."

"Immature maybe, but it worked – oh what joy it was watching him being tossed out of the room. No one suspected it was me all along."

Candy was not amused. "Vulcan, *I* knew it was you. I think you should just drop it. Face it, old friend: Lupo is here to stay."

Vulcan sprung into a vicious growl and stood over Candy. "DON'T YOU EVER SAY THAT AGAIN! LUPO IS AS GOOD AS GONE!"

Candy was used to Vulcan's rage. "Vulcan, I suggest you get that temper under control before we have to go for the official birthday portrait. The nation won't want to see a miserable dorgi. Remember, we present a united front for the people of this great nation. Today is an historic day and I, for one, am not letting your scheming get in the way of a full eclipse *and* cake!"

As much as Vulcan hated to admit it, Candy was right. Today was not the day to get distracted by Lupo. All the Queen's dogs would be included in the official photograph and he wanted the entire world to see Her Majesty Queen Elizabeth II sitting next to Vulcan, the rightful King of all the animals of the United Kingdom.

Kicking the pink bone towards Monty, who was fast asleep and snoring so loudly he sounded like a wild hog, Vulcan checked what the footmen were serving to the birthday guests. Silver trays of the tastiest roast beef and potatoes, Yorkshire puddings and succulent honey-glazed carrots were carefully carried by palace servants dressed in clean white trousers and smart black waistcoats.

There was still time before Vulcan needed to be

in the Throne Room for the official birthday portrait with the family. Time enough for him to duck out and discover what Lupo was up to. He saw the royal spaniel once more and muttered menacingly under his breath, "Strange things can happen during an eclipse . . ."

Lupo was scratching the skirting board, trying to find an opening in the wall big enough to squeeze through, when Holly found him.

"What are you up to?" she asked as he pawed at the beautiful hand-painted wood.

"Two palace mice just ran through here. They were talking about a hidden room." Lupo sniffed the air again, hoping to pick up a clue as to where they may have gone. "We have to find them."

"Lupo, there are *hundreds* of mice in the palace. We are never going to find them. Even if you could sniff them out, we're triple the size. We wouldn't be able to follow them. Palace mice are able to squeeze into ridiculously small holes and this house has quite a few gaps they could get through!"

"We need Herbert. I wish he was here with us."

Holly was concerned. "Lupo, I still don't

understand what the big hurry is. Queen Ebony has been dead for thousands of years. No one found her in all the years she's been lost. So what makes you so sure you are going to find her now?"

"No one was looking for her then. *Everyone* is looking for her now," he replied.

"Look, they will be taking the Queen's birthday photograph shortly and I'm expected to be in it," said Holly, seeing a queasy-looking photographer sitting uncomfortably on a chair at the end of the hallway waiting to be escorted to the Throne Room.

Lupo thought fast. He wouldn't have Holly's help for much longer. If he was going to explore Buckingham Palace he needed a map. Then he had an idea. "Holly, you know the map of entrances and exits to the palace? The one on the Red route." Holly nodded so Lupo continued, "Do you think all the entrances are still in use? I could probably get a really good look around if I used them to explore different parts of the palace."

Holly smiled. "Great plan! I never thought to use Eos's map. If you want to stay hidden it's really the only way to get around. But you're also right, if you follow the map you'll be able to check off parts of

Buckingham Palace pretty quickly. You can cross off the Commoners' Pantry – it's been blocked for a while now."

"Why's that?" asked Lupo, curious.

"Not sure – it's the oldest entrance. It's used as some kind of storage room. Very dusty and full of old junk."

"Storage room, you say . . ." Lupo's senses were on alert; something telling him that the pantry required further investigation.

"Yes," she said, noticing Lupo's tail wagging, which he did only when he was on to something.

"Thanks, Holly! See you later and don't forget to say 'cheese'!" said Lupo, before hurrying on his way.

Vulcan was standing behind a plinth outside the Hall. He had only just made it out to hear the last bit of Lupo and Holly's discussion. "So we are *all* looking for that hidden room," he said in a hushed whisper.

He watched as Lupo said his goodbyes to Holly and then bounded off down the corridor towards the King's Study. He made a mental note to block off all three of the study's entry points. He'd get to work on it the first chance he could, he needed to restrict everyone's access to Buckingham Palace – particularly Lupo's.

Kitty and Herbert arrived at the Commoners' Pantry entrance to Buckingham Palace. Herbert was sure that it was the best place for them to start their search for Ebony. Kitty pushed hard on the entrance. It refused to budge. She tried again and again.

"Come on, Kitty, put your back into it! PUSH!" demanded Herbert.

Eventually she managed to get in. Pushing the door open, they waited to let their eyes adjust to the darkness. They saw that the room was full of old garden furniture. There were boxes piled high together with all sorts of royal bric-a-brac. Herbert bounced on to an old Victorian child's trike.

"If you ask me, someone blocked up that door deliberately," said Kitty, dusting off her paws.

"Vulcan," said an exhausted Herbert. "I wonder why he'd go to all the trouble of blocking up this doorway? Most odd. I will send a team in to inspect. These entrance points must be kept clear at all times."

Kitty looked around the room. "I don't think I

have ever been in here before. Look at all this stuff – this newspaper is old. *Really* old."

Herbert jumped on to Kitty's back and ran all the way to her tabby shoulder to get a better look at the front page of the paper. "You're right. See, the year is 1862. Buckingham Palace looked very different back then."

Kitty peered more closely at the picture of the imposing building, blackened and stained from the days when London's streets were all smog and chimney soot. "That's just some old London building. It's not Buckingham Palace. Looks nothing like it!" she declared.

"That's what it looked like before the works were completed to change the East Front – pretty different! They completely rebuilt the front of the palace. I seem to recall seeing a report on mice conditions at the time. Here's an interesting fact – it said that the palace mice preferred to live outside before the works were completed. Can you believe it? They would rather sleep in the snow than be inside the palace!" Herbert continued, "The East Front rebuilding programme was so successful that the mice finally felt safe enough to move back in. Many mice made their home between the new palace and the old."

"Palace mice sleeping outside?" challenged Kitty. "That can't be right!"

"No, it's true. Maybe something scared them *inside* the palace?"

Kitty looked around again. Her green eyes glowed. "Where are we again?"

"The Commoners' Pantry," replied Herbert.

"The oldest part of the palace."

Herbert ran around, inspecting the floorboards and feeling the walls. "If I am not mistaken this is part of the original palace before the works. Yes, yes, I am sure of it."

"So no human has been in here for years . . ." whistled Kitty.

"Indeed. Doesn't look like it judging by the level of dust," said Herbert, sneezing loudly.

Kitty walked further into the room. There was a faint glow from the far end.

"Kitty, wait – where are you going? Watch out for that!" shouted Herbert, trying to keep up with the curious tabby. A box fell, and Victorian children's books spilled out all over the floor. "This isn't safe! I must insist we get back. We won't be able to access the palace through here. It's just too full of stuff!"

But Kitty wasn't listening. She was walking deeper in to the darkness.

"KITTY, WHAT ON EARTH ARE YOU DOING?"

"I think I know why all those old mice preferred to sleep outside rather than be in here," she purred, sniffing the humid air.

"Why?" said Herbert, manoeuvering clumsily over the books.

"You were right, something in the palace *did* scare them out, " she said, cryptically. "I don't hear or see any mice in here. Don't you think that's a little strange? I mean, isn't this room perfect for them?"

"Nothing scares palace mice . . . Oh . . . except . . ." Herbert hushed himself.

"There is nothing scarier to a mouse than a *cat* . . ." answered Kitty.

Herbert looked around in wonder. "You don't think that . . ."

Kitty nodded in the dark, her body going into stealth mode. "Herbert, I'm so convinced I am willing to bet my last fish supper that *this* is where Ebony is."

Holly watched as the Queen made her way up to the state rooms. Willow and Candy were trotting along next to Her Majesty's pink calves. Her sensible blue leather shoes creaked as she headed up the main staircase. Her handbag swung on her left arm, which meant that the doggy treats would be in the palm of her right hand, normally wrapped in a folded handkerchief.

Tommy the footman narrowly avoided tripping over Holly as he picked up his pace, trying to keep up with Her Majesty's swift steps. The rest of the royal family trailed behind. Three ladies' maids carried the heavy hand-woven silk and velvet Robe of State. Holly giggled to herself as she saw Prince George's little hands reaching out trying to grab at the robe's silky crown and ER symbol.

At the door to the Throne Room, two more footmen bowed and silently opened a pair of tall white doors and the full splendour and magnificence inside was revealed. This room was used for ceremonial receptions. Holly saw the pride on the faces of the palace servants as they watched their Queen making her way solemnly towards her throne. Two men with large swords stood guard over a large leather box, which was resting on a table near the Queen.

Holly bent down so her short nose touched the floor. The old rug beneath her smelt like it had been covered in flowers at some point. Her blue eyes narrowed as she looked up and focused on the golden woodwork in the ceiling. Light from outside shone through the clean windows on to the heavy red and gold curtains. It bounced off tall mirrors and an impressive triple set of crystal chandeliers. The brilliant red walls seemed to glow more brightly now that the Queen was there.

As the princes and princesses and dukes and duchesses found their seats, the ladies' maids carefully draped the Robe of State around Her Majesty's shoulders. No one said a word as the leather box next to her was carefully unclicked.

Prince George saw it first. Holly noticed his brilliant brown eyes light up. Sitting on a large red velvet cushion near him was the Imperial State Crown. Hundreds of smaller diamonds were overshadowed by an impressively large collection of ancient jewels. Its centre stone was a large red ruby. One of Her Majesty's ladies-in-waiting carefully picked up the crown and carried it to the Queen on her throne, stopping briefly to smile at Holly.

Monty yawned sleepily as he and Willow made themselves comfortable to the left and right of the Queen's blue shoes. Candy, who was late and still clutching her bone, scampered forwards between the Prince's feet, making excuses for her tardy behaviour.

"BONE," Willow said, reminding Candy that she had the half-chewed bone hanging out of her mouth.

"Indeed, sorry, sorry," said Candy, dropping the mangled bone at one of the footmen's feet as she scrabbled into place on the step directly below Monty.

Holly saw that Vulcan was missing. She looked around just in time to see him slip in via a side door.

He regarded Holly in a strange, knowing way. She watched as he pompously trotted up the steps that led up to the throne and sat directly in front of the Queen.

The Duchess ruffled the top of Holly's head as she walked around the family's chairs and made her way up the throne stairs to her normal place on the middle step, directly to the left of the throne. Prince George *gurgled* merrily, because he liked being around the family.

Everyone watched as the Queen placed the crown on her head.

The photographer adjusted his camera as rays of warm sunshine poured into the throne room, covering the entire royal family in a warm glow. Everyone sat waiting, ready for the birthday portrait to be taken. Outside the palace, the clouds drifted away, leaving a brilliantly clear sky. Crowds gathered in the royal park in the afternoon sunshine, waiting to witness the full eclipse of the sun.

Meanwhile, underneath the palace, Lupo studied Eos's map. The Commoners' Pantry seemed like a logical place to start his hunt for the hidden room.

He followed the Red route to the entrance – and wasn't disappointed when he arrived. Dusty footprints on the carpet revealed that a mouse and a cat had recently been to the doorway. Holly had said that the route in had been blocked. "Herbert and Kitty," he said hopefully.

Lupo pushed against a small wooden door and found that it opened easily. Whatever had been blocking it was now gone. It was too dark to see anything beyond his front paws, but immediately he picked up two familiar smells. Putting his nose to the floor, he took in a deep breath. But the combination of heat, dust and what smelled like old wood dulled his senses. It was no good – he had no idea which direction his friends had gone. His long black ears pricked up to see if he could detect anything.

"I thought I heard the unmistakable sound of a dog sniffing," said Herbert.

"*Herbert!* I'm very happy to see you. What are you doing in here?" asked Lupo. His left paw began to tingle as he picked up a strong vibration from inside the room. Something heavy was moving across the floor.

"If my navigational skills are correct, the Commoners' Pantry is the oldest part of the palace . . ." Herbert began.

"And you think this is where Ebony is?" said Lupo excitedly. "*This* is the hidden room, isn't it?"

"Quite possibly. Kitty is here with me – we are looking for Bertie's cargo. I think it is of the utmost importance that we find it before the eclipse," said Herbert.

"That's it – it's today's eclipse. *That's* what will wake her up!" Lupo said, shocked.

"Yes," said Kitty from the top of a box high above them. In the darkness the tabby could easily have been mistaken for a black cat. She jumped down with ease and landed next to her two friends. "Lupo, there is every chance she will wake up once the sun is hidden behind the moon, and once she is awake we won't be able to stop her taking her revenge." Kitty then paused, seeing Lupo's face. "It's the curse we all need to be worried about."

Lupo whispered to himself, "The curse of eternal sleep."

Kitty explained: "If Ebony rises, she will send the entire royal family to sleep. That is what the curse means."

Herbert began to shake all over. His glasses bounced around on the end of his nose. Kitty tugged on Herbert's green cardigan with one paw and with the other she put her paw up to her lips. "Sssshhhh! Enough with all that rattling."

All of a sudden, the wheel of a child's trike started to turn all on its own. A strange sliding noise was all around them as something was dragged along the floor. Lupo growled more loudly. He was keen to protect his friends from whatever was making its way towards them. Ahead of him he could see boxes shuddering and moving. "Whatever it is, it's heading this way," Lupo whispered loudly, his voice was strong and courageous.

Kitty tried to listen but she was distracted by a loud rattling. She sneered. "Herbert. Stop shaking so much."

Lupo looked over and saw that Herbert wasn't moving at all. "It's not him. That rattling is from whatever is coming towards *us*."

Just as Herbert turned to see what was behind him, something grabbed him. It began to squeeze him tight. He tried to shout out, to warn Lupo and

Kitty but it was no good.

"Hiss!" it said.

It was too late – it had Herbert. Slowly, Lupo and Kitty turned to face the creature that had them surrounded. A huge, terrifying cobra stood in a pool of pale light. Its blackened skin looked like it was locked together with the links of a chain. It had a small face, balanced on top of a neck that fanned outwards and its eyes blinked quickly and sharply as it watched the petrified palace animals. A small sculpture of what appeared to be a cat made of solid gold rested on the top of its head. Long strands of turquoise and gold beads hung off the edge of it. They snapped together sharply as its long body entwined itself yet more tightly around Herbert's furry brown midriff.

Lupo felt the courage rise in him. He was not about to let the snake attack his friends without a fight, nor was he going to let an ancient cat take over! He had to protect his family.

"Let him go!" he said calmly, his bravery glimmering out of his brown eyes.

The snake bared a pair of huge fangs, its mouth agape, as it held Herbert tightly in its grip. It hissed, warning Lupo and Kitty to come no closer.

"PUT HIM DOWN!" screamed Kitty.

Lupo peered at the snake closely. "Kitty, it's not going to hurt him," Lupo said confidently. "It's warning us. I think it's trying to get us to leave."

Lupo was right! Kitty saw that the snake was no longer squeezing their friend. Herbert was wriggling free. The snake slithered nearer and stared into Kitty's eyes, as if bewitched by the palace cat. When it was ready, it released Herbert. Finally, its tail stopped rattling and it slithered away, leaving them all safe but puzzled.

Kitty was dazed. "It stared into my eyes and spoke to me." She looked fearfully at her friends. "It spoke in a strange language. I couldn't understand at first, but I *went* somewhere with it – somewhere beyond this room to a much earlier time. I could see water, and a river full of animals. I could see hippos and herons. They were happily singing and I was waving and rejoicing . . ." Kitty stopped herself, afraid to continue.

Herbert adjusted his cardigan,

re-aligning all his buttons. "It sounds to me like that snake wanted you to see where it came from. You said that there were hippos and a river?" He looked quickly between Lupo and Kitty. "My dear Kitty, I think you were looking at the River Nile. I think you were in ancient Egypt!"

Kitty looked frightened, asking them both: "How's that possible?"

Lupo looked around the dark room. "I don't know, but Prince George is upstairs and I'm not about to have some great big cobra scaring him."

Herbert's little watch chimed. "The moon is going to pass over the sun shortly. We don't have long to find Ebony before she wakes. Lupo, you must leave, I absolutely insist! According to my files, Ebony will wake up at the very moment of the eclipse. The first thing she will do is drain the power from a dog, since it was a dog that dragged her to the afterlife. It will be her first act of revenge. When she has enough power she will put everyone to sleep using her sacred rattle. The curse at Buckingham Palace can't be allowed to spread to the rest of the world."

"I'm not leaving. I have to stop this before the eclipse. The snake went *that* way. It must be down here guarding Ebony's sarcophagus."

They started walking, and every step they took felt to Lupo like going further back in time. The cobra had a faint but definite smell, like old paper and fragrant oils. He inhaled deeply. "We are getting closer. The smell is getting stronger."

Lupo gritted his teeth as they arrived at a set of very old looking wooden crates marked "BY SEA" and "VR". The last stamp on the boxes made it clear what they had found:

CARIO, EGYPT *to* BUCKINGHAM PALACE, LONDON, ENGLAND
PRIVATE PROPERTY OF VICTORIA REGINA

* * *

The photographer was finally relaxing, now that Her Majesty's official birthday portrait was complete. After the final click, the private secretary politely informed the family that the best view of the full eclipse would be from the yellow living room, which was also where the afternoon's birthday party would take place.

Holly had watched Vulcan sitting in front of the

camera, enjoying his moment in the spotlight a little too much. But he was gone before the Queen's crown had been removed.

Once the Imperial Crown was carefully placed back into the large leather box, Her Majesty clicked open her handbag to remove a large white handkerchief. Praising each dog for their service, she gave each of them a tasty treat.

Holly bowed to the throne. She looked around at her large family, all of whom she loved dearly. She loved them as much as she loved Lupo, who at that very same moment was staring at a large golden mask of a long lost ancient cat.

8
Ebony's Eclipse

Vulcan had found the photographer weak and uninspiring. He had taken some "experimental" pictures of the family in the past and they were met with "immense satisfaction," according to the palace press office. Long gone were those early years when he would sit comfortably at the feet of the monarch and the photographer would concentrate on trying to capture the very spirit of the Queen. No, today it was all "big smiles" and "natural light".

As he headed for the main staircase, Vulcan promised himself that he would force back his feelings of annoyance and focus on the task in hand. He had to find Queen Ebony before anyone else got to her. He had learnt a great deal sitting in the King's Study, night after night, as the Queen's husband read and reread Bertie's scribbly journals. The Duke would read aloud, hoping the words would slot into place like pieces of a jigsaw puzzle.

Vulcan had sat up when he had finally pieced everything together himself. Bertie, according to his last journal, had not been well after clearing out the cave. He wrote that a large cobra had bitten him. Then he'd slept for days, and although he didn't dream, his mind was full of an inky blackness. He woke only as the last of the precious objects were loaded on to camels and carried away to the ship bound for Queen Victoria in London.

At long last freed from the darkness, he wrote: I woke to find that my instructions to send the cave's contents to Mother in England had been completed. I wonder what she will make of the feline Queen?

It was obvious to Vulcan that the tomb's contents contained some kind of ancient curse because the captain's logs from the ship had said that a great black cobra had attacked the crew en route to England. The captain wrote that he had been inspecting Queen Victoria's cargo when he had been bitten and had, like Bertie, fallen into a deep sleep. He'd woken to

111

find the snake loose on the ship. When they eventually caught it they put it in a box. Then he instructed that all the Prince's mysterious cargo should be loaded on to a smaller boat and dragged behind the tall steam ship – just in case there were other snakes lurking within the items.

Once safely docked in Britain, the contents had been sent on to Buckingham Palace. The last thing the captain wrote was that he was pleased to see the back of the cargo and that thankfully no more snakes had been found.

Having reached his conclusions, Vulcan's plan had come together nicely. He would find Ebony and wake her up. Then, he would command her to put the entire palace to sleep so that he could take over.

Not even Vulcan could have realized just how foolish his plan was.

The family made their way from the throne room to the Queen's special yellow living room, which ran alongside the gardens. Everyone was in good spirits, looking forward to the rare eclipse.

Lupo was hiding behind a large blue vase in the

hallway, waiting for a glimpse of Prince George. He didn't have to wait long. Nanny was dutifully pushing the little buggy down the hallway. When she stopped to smell the large display of fresh flowers in the blue vase, Lupo took the opportunity to jump into the buggy.

Lupo licked the side of George's face. "Wake up, George, wake up!"

The toddler opened his brown eyes and smiled. "Lupo!" he mumbled loudly.

"SSSSSHHHHH!" Lupo pawed at the prince's tiny ear. "I have to get you out of here, buddy. I've found something bad in the Commoners' Pantry . . ."

Nanny pushed the buggy forward, past the grandfather clock, as she headed for the living room. The family were putting on their safety goggles to watch the solar event. Then they gathered at the windows. Lupo was watching from underneath the tiny blankets in George's buggy. The eclipse was only a matter of minutes away.

High in the sky the moon swung into view. A hush fell amongst the family as they waited. Slowly, the circles of the sun began to merge, and the sky turned dark. The trees stopped moving and the birds ceased their happy tweeting. Squirrels in the royal gardens climbed down from their branches and ran for their homes. Ducks in the palace's lake dived under lily pads and the fish underneath the royal water swam as deep as they could. Soon nothing stirred.

The sun was gone and Buckingham Palace was cloaked in darkness.

Kaye and Charlotte were exactly where Vulcan guessed they would be in the banqueting hall. The two mice were as thick as thieves and had gained quite a reputation for causing mayhem amongst the others. Whilst everyone was watching the eclipse, they were sharing a thimble of very expensive champagne.

"I told you it was there!" said Charlotte.

"A new home!" Kaye danced on her spindly legs.

"Whoop, whoop!" said Charlotte. "Just think of all the parties we could have in there!"

Vulcan took this as his cue. "How lovely it is to see you again, Kaye and Charlotte! New home, you say? And where might this be? Not in the 'lost room' or what did you call it? 'The hidden room'?"

he asked, his whiskers twitching.

The two mice were quite shocked to find that the royal dorgi had been spying on them. "Hey! How do you know about that?" squeaked Charlotte.

"Let's just say I hear what I need to hear when I need to hear it. Where is this room?"

"Kaye, don't tell him!" demanded Charlotte.

Kaye shook, afraid of what Vulcan might do if she didn't tell him. "It's in the Commoners' Pantry," she blurted, not wanting any trouble.

Vulcan's mouth curled. "Not a hidden room . . . just a dusty old storeroom, then." He had been there only a few days ago to block it off with an old box. How he could have missed the hoard languishing within was beyond him.

Charlotte was off like a rocket. Vulcan raced after her, calling, "Charlotte, don't think I can't keep up with you!"

Kaye trailed behind, doing her best to keep up with the tiny brown mouse and the royal dorgi who were now racing through the palace towards the Commoners' Pantry.

Herbert and Kitty were arguing as to which box to

hide behind when Charlotte burst into the room, looking more than a little stressed.

"What are you lot doing in here?" she said, jumping in their way. "Those boxes belong to Kaye and me! That's our home! First Vulcan, now you two! Who's next?"

Herbert had never seen such a fine-looking brown mouse. "I'm sorry . . . did you say Vulcan?"

"Yes! He's right behind me. Get out, all of you! Put that box down! I found it. It belongs to me!" said Charlotte, putting her foot down.

Kitty bent down, her nose resting on the floor, her eyes level with the little rocket. "Where is Vulcan?" said the palace tabby, looking around.

"I'm right here," said Vulcan, slipping into the room behind them, followed by Lupo.

"Vulcan, we all have to leave, it's not safe," he panted, trying to catch his breath.

Kitty ran to his side. "What about Prince George?"

Lupo winked to his friends. "He's safely tucked away with Nanny. He started crying just as everything went dark. Nanny took him upstairs to the playroom. It's as far away as I could get him."

Vulcan laughed. "You are pathetic, Lupo – you

and that baby always whispering away in corners, with no one understanding a word of what you're saying. I don't know what is worse, you being a member of my family or you talking to that baby."

Lupo stood firm. He growled loudly. "Vulcan, get out. It's not safe for you in here."

"Safe for me? I think it is you who should be worried. Your little band of merry soldiers can't stop a thing. You poor creatures, I shall enjoy seeing you sleep for all eternity. Terrible pity, you'll all miss out on my coronation. Perhaps I will have Ebony wake you for it . . . Hmmm."

Lupo ignored Vulcan's jibes. "Ebony will hurt us all. She is a *cat,* Vulcan; an ancient one at that. I don't think she will take kindly to any of us being anywhere near her."

Vulcan bared his sharp little teeth. "Grrr – be gone! This is my PALACE! EBONY belongs to ME!"

Charlotte looked frantically around. She was stranded between two dogs that were poised for battle, a tabby cat that looked like it could swallow her in one bite and the Head of MI5, who was looking at her like he was in love. Suddenly, they all seemed to gaze in her direction and shrink away. "Yes, that's right, clear off, all of you!" she said confidently, believing that she had successfully got rid of the intruders – until she saw the cobra behind her.

The cobra wasn't alone. Standing either side of it were two great big sphinxes cloaked in gold. The room then filled with a deafening roar.

Kitty stepped back, anxious at what might be coming next. She shouted, "The eclipse must be nearly over. WE HAVE TO GET OUT OF HERE. THIS ISN'T GOOD!"

Vulcan had no intention of leaving.

The entire room began to shake. Boxes began falling to the floor and splitting open, their contents pouring out everywhere. Lupo was convinced he could feel sand under his paws. Just then, a bright glow shone out from around a large box. The lid shot through the air and hit the ground, shattering into a thousand splinters.

"WE NEED TO LEAVE!" cried Kitty.

Charlotte was hiding behind Herbert. "What's that?" she squeaked nervously.

Green eyes flashed all around the glowing box as several other sphinxes appeared.

Herbert said, "There are more now . . . and they

don't look too happy to see us."

Lupo scooped up both mice putting them on his back "GUYS, HANG ON. KITTY, RUN!" he said, not wanting to look back.

Vulcan stood waiting. The box moved uneasily. *Something* was inside it. The large stone sphinxes with their magnificent eyes gathered around the edge of the box and carefully removed the golden cat mask. Vulcan eyed the treasure hungrily. Emeralds as green as fresh grass glinted in the light, diamonds the size of his paws nestled in the pointy golden ears and a solid red ruby sat on the end of its nose. This was a cat mask like no other.

The black cobra slipped into the box. *This* was it. The moment he had been waiting for. The loud roaring was abating. Sand fell all about him.

Vulcan lost his breath momentarily as an elegant-looking black cat rose out of the box. The golden mask was an exact replica of her exquisite feline features. She blinked with huge green eyes that seemed to look right through him. "Goodnight, little doggy," she purred.

* * *

Lupo, Kitty, Herbert and Charlotte stood in the middle of the Red route. The sheer force of Ebony's rising had upset everything, such as the pictures which had fallen off the walls.

"It was my home and now it's gone," said Charlotte sadly.

Lupo gave the tiny mouse the comfort of his left paw. "I'm sorry, Charlotte. I am sure I can find you and Kaye a nice home at Kensington Palace. I don't think *that* particular home was suitable – too many cats . . ."

"And one giant snake!" said Kitty, cleaning the dust and sand out of her tabby fur.

Herbert gathered his thoughts. "Vulcan is still in there."

Lupo was concerned too. "Herbert, you need to get back to MI5 and warn your team – no, warn *all* the mice. We don't know what Ebony is capable of and frankly, I am not looking forward to seeing who or what she is. If this curse is real we'll have little time to stop it. We're going to need everyone's help."

Kitty was rooted to the spot. She knew exactly who the ancient cat was and she also knew what it was planning on doing. Now that Ebony was awake,

there was little time to act.

Herbert bounced off, taking Charlotte with him so that they could warn as many mice as they could about the sudden arrival of a very dark and old Buckingham Palace cat.

Lupo started to head back into the pantry when Kitty stopped him. "What are you going to do?"

"Do you remember when we first met you said that cats and dogs can't be friends?"

Kitty nodded, remembering how she had spent days trying to think of a good enough reason not to be friends with the Duke and Duchess's dog.

Lupo continued: "Well, I figure this is the same thing."

Kitty shook her head. "Lupo, this isn't the same thing at all. Ebony was a goddess in her day. She has the power to change the world. It's not safe – how many dogs do you see in books on ancient Egypt?"

Lupo shrugged. "Not many."

"Precisely," said Kitty, satisfied she was finally getting through to him. "Ebony had all the dogs sent away."

Lupo smiled. "Are you telling me that it's because of Ebony that you thought we couldn't be friends?"

Kitty smiled back. "That's right."

"Look, Kitty, as much as I dislike Vulcan, I can't leave him alone to face her and her army of cats. He needs me." With that, walked back into the pantry.

"Well, you are not going in there alone," she said. "That cat doesn't know what it's like inside a prince's dirty laundry! Believe me, that cat hasn't got a clue what she's waking up to."

9
Ebony is Rattled

Lupo coughed. The room was filled with a fine dust. It swirled in places, as if stirred up by something large. The room was also lighter, as if a light had been turned on somewhere.

Kitty asked, "Is it me or has it suddenly got really dusty in here?" She stroked her eyelids and then her whiskers clean.

It wasn't *just* dusty. Lupo could feel heat, which made him more nervous. The entire room grew warmer. As they got further in, the room got even lighter and hotter. Under their paws the floorboards began to disappear and in their place they felt soft, warm sand.

"What's happening?" asked Kitty nervously.

Lupo's worst fears were confirmed. "I don't think

we are in Buckingham Palace anymore," he said.

Overhead, a blazing sun beat down on their fur coats. All around them were sandy dunes.

"Where *are* we?" asked Kitty, looking at a large pyramid directly in front of them.

"If I didn't know it was impossible, I'd say we were in ancient Egypt," said Lupo.

Two giant sphinxes walked alongside them, carrying spears of gold.

"Those two weren't here a minute ago—" Kitty sharpened her gaze "—and over there. Isn't that Vulcan?"

The dorgi was sitting motionless on a stone plinth. Lupo walked up to him. "Vulcan, quick, get down – we have to—" But it was no good. Vulcan was in a dreamless sleep.

When Lupo turned back, Kitty too was motionless, rooted to the spot. His eyes looked over to the black cat that was walking to them.

Kitty whispered, "Whatever you do, don't say a word. Leave this to me."

Ebony circled them, like an eagle checking out her prey. An elephant, a hippo and a heron all dressed in robes of gold and white cotton took their places around her. Solemnly the animals dropped their heads. Kitty did the same.

Lupo stared into Ebony's emerald-coloured eyes. She looked in every way like a normal black cat, apart from the fine gold bangles around her paws, the elaborate necklace round her neck and the solid gold crown on her head. He could hear her whisper in his mind: "Lupo, the royal dog . . . Well, well, well. A long time ago, I ruled over the world and then I was dragged to the underworld by a DOG just like YOU!" She was clearly toying with what to do with him. Her long, slender paw pointed to Vulcan's plinth. "Thanks to Vulcan, my powers are almost entirely restored. Before I sent him to the darkness I had a good look around his mind. VULCAN, the dog with big plans! He actually thought he could rule!"

Her gaze landed on the hippo's face. "YOU'RE STARING AT YOUR QUEEN. I may have been asleep for a thousand years but I have not forgotten RESPECT. YOU could learn respect from LUPO. He is a dog with honour. Only minutes before I was awoken he was off squirrelling away a human prince." She turned to address all the assembled company. "FIND THE BABY and bring it to ME. GO! ALL

OF YOU LAZY ANIMALS, GO!"

Lupo's paws began to shake. He hoped Prince George was upstairs in the playroom with Nanny.

The ancient cat spoke: "Lupo, *I* SEE YOU. I can feel the fear wrapping itself around your mind." Her snake reappeared behind Vulcan and hissed angrily in agreement. "YOU HAVE NO POWER, LUPO. What's that you are saying? 'I will stop you!' Sweet the little spaniel thinks it can take on the likes of me! A QUEEN. I WILL CRUSH YOU FIRST. I WILL TAKE EVERY ONE OF YOUR NICE MEMORIES AND I WILL LEAVE YOU EMPTY TO SWIM IN DARKNESS! YOU have no idea of the incredible powers I will soon possess."

Lupo growled. Ebony was inside his head, raiding his memories – those joyous times spent with George in the nursery. He tried his hardest to push her out, but it didn't work. His thoughts turned cloudy and dark. He suddenly felt very sad.

"Do I send you into the darkness?" Ebony said merrily.

Lupo looked defiantly at her. She continued to assess him; her eyes doing all the talking. Lupo watched them narrow as she considered his fate.

They closed and opened once more, which meant she seemed to have made a decision. Her green eyes widened.

"Ah, not yet . . . you might be useful. Yes. You're frightened of me. That is good. You have a strong heart, LUPO, but a weak mind. YOU WILL DO AS I BID or I will never release your precious Prince George."

Out of the corner of his eyes Lupo could see Kitty. She still wasn't moving. Several large crocodiles now surrounded her. "Please don't hurt her . . ." he blurted.

Ebony's head dropped to one side as if she was once again trying to reach a decision. Lupo heard the black cat in his head. "FIND THE RATTLE."

A strange, dark mist descended. Lupo blinked, hoping to see Kitty still, but she was gone. He closed his eyes to protect them from the swirling sands that filled the air. When he opened them, Ebony and her army had disappeared and Kitty was lying on the floor next to him. They were back in the room in the Palace, broken boxes lying all around them.

He nudged Kitty awake. "Kitty, are you OK?"

Kitty put both paws over his. "I'm awake. Please

tell me that it's safe to open my eyes."

"It's OK. We're back," he said.

"Lupo, she spoke to me – I mean, I heard her inside my head." Kitty steadied herself. "She told me to find a rattle. We have to do as she says."

Lupo nodded. "Whatever it is must be pretty important because she said the same thing to me. I'm going to try and get George to safety. Don't give up on me just yet. Ebony thinks she can rule but she's forgetting this is a very different time and she doesn't have the friends we have."

"But if we don't find this rattle, then what?" asked Kitty nervously.

Lupo went very silent, thinking. He needed to find out what this rattle was and what it meant to Ebony. A plan began to form.

"Kitty, you need to tell me everything you know about Ebony – I mean, everything. I know you know more about her than you are letting on. I need to know where she came from. She must have had an enemy? Or—"

Kitty interrupted him. "Shhusssshhh! Look, I don't know why Ebony needs that rattle. All I know is that she is not to be messed with. We have to evacuate the palace before she starts putting everyone to sleep. Can we please just get out of here!"

As they left neither of them saw the huge back cobra quietly watching. "*Hiss.*"

Holly found Lupo and Kitty on the main staircase. "What's wrong?" she said.

Lupo was pleased to see Holly. He said, "Let's just say I'm re-thinking everything I learnt about Egypt. I don't think it was a fun place at all."

"Who said Egypt was fun? I always thought it sounded awfully hot – not a place for a royal dog."

Kitty grabbed Lupo and planted herself on the staircase. "That's *IT*! Noble – he was Ebony's enemy. He was the dog that dragged her to the underworld. You have to find him. I remember Matilda telling me all about him when I was a kitten!"

"Noble? That's odd," said Holly. "Queen Victoria had a dog called Noble. He never left her side. The history books say that she described him as her one true companion after Prince Albert died. Could it be the same dog?"

"Is it even possible?" queried Lupo.

"He'd be very old!" mused Holly. "There are a

couple of paintings of him here in the palace. There is a big one in the Egyptian room."

"Egyptian room!" asked Lupo and Kitty together.

"Queen Victoria was passionate about Noble *and* about Egypt. She created a room for them both upstairs, full of the treasures given to her from the ancient world. But I am not going to take you there until you tell me what on earth is going on!"

"Ebony is awake . . ." Kitty told Holly what they had seen. "She wants a golden rattle and she's sent her guardians off to find Prince George. We don't have long – soon she will be able to put every human to sleep. We have to get the rest of the family out of here."

Holly resisted any idea of evacuating the family. "Lupo, it's the Queen's birthday. You, of all dogs, have to understand we can't just burst in on the celebrations – besides, how on earth would we get them all out? They would sooner remove us for causing a disturbance!"

Lupo smiled into her eyes, and she knew exactly what he was thinking. "Oh, hang on a minute," she said. "If we cause enough of a disturbance they will be forced out of the celebrations."

132

"My thoughts exactly. Only thing is – it needs to be something BIG," he muttered.

Kitty thought for a minute and then said, "What about an invasion?"

Lupo looked at Kitty, then speaking to them both, said, "That's it, Kitty! We need cats. And lots of them."

"You think that will work?" queried Kitty.

"Yes! It's a great idea – the Queen can't bear cats! But we are going to need a lot of them if we are going to stand the tiniest chance of your plan working, Lupo," said Holly with satisfaction.

Lupo shook his head. "The first problem is that we don't *know* any cats other than Kitty and, second, are you *sure* the Queen doesn't like cats?"

Kitty had an answer. "When it comes to getting cats in the palace, leave that to me. Second, I never told either of you this, but once I did actually run into the Queen and I have never seen a human so scared."

Lupo was having second thoughts. "Is this the best we can come up with?"

Holly shrugged. "By the sounds of it, we don't have much time to find this rattle, and the only way

133

we can keep everyone safe is to get the royal family out of here. I think it's a good plan. I'm not sure the Queen *is* scared of cats but I know she's terrified of mice – aren't all humans?"

"Oh hang on – I had a mouse in my mouth at the time . . ." said Kitty. "Maybe she was scared of the mouse and not me . . ."

A loud trumpet sounded downstairs, signalling the start of Her Majesty's birthday party in the living room.

Lupo took charge. "Kitty, get as many cats as possible to flood the Palace. Holly and I need to get to Prince George then I think you had better take me to that Egyptian room of Queen Victoria's."

Kitty agreed to do her best at rounding up as many cats as possible. "Leave it to me," she said. "This should be a piece of cake!"

Beneath the main staircase, the famous Buckingham Palace kitchens were buzzing with the news that the cake was ready. In the Head Pastry Chef's office, the other chef, Morris, celebrated whilst dancing to "Walk Like an Egyptian" by the Bangles. Adjusting his chef's hat and smoothing down his moustache, he decided he was very happy with all his hard work.

"Happy Birthday Elizabeth II" was carefully piped on top of the finest carrot cake in navy blue royal icing. Handmade sugary flowers, horses and painted corgis and even a miniature Lupo had been delicately arranged around the cake's three perfect red, blue and white buttercream tiers. It was a masterpiece that had taken Morris six long weeks to create. The kitchen staff all clapped when he announced that it was complete.

"And now comes the easy bit!" said the delighted chef, relieved and exhausted. "All we have to do is get it up to the living room and wheel it in for the Queen!"

Matilda picked up one of her paws and inspected the state of her claws while Burmese munched on a long bit of sugary hay.

"Something's up. I can feel it in my tummy," said Matilda. "I am hoping it's not what I think it is . . ." worried the wise grey cat.

Burmese was ready for a carrot. Poking her head out of her stable, she watched as Kitty made her way towards her. "Hello, Kitty!"

Kitty leapt high up on to the ledge of the royal

stables. Politely she said, "Burmese, it's always such a pleasure to see you. Sorry it's not a longer visit. Have you seen my aunt? It's very urgent that I speak with her."

"She's right back there," Burmese replied. "Go ahead, little one – but watch out, something's got her all in a tangle."

Kitty found Matilda hiding under a big pile of straw. "I'M NOT HERE!" she meowed.

"I can see you. This isn't the time for games. I need your help and I need it fast. We have to save the royal family," Kitty pleaded.

"Come back and see me in the morning!" purred Matilda.

"There may not be a tomorrow at all. Ebony is already awake," replied Kitty.

"WHAT!" Matilda shot out of her straw bed. "SAY THAT AGAIN!"

Kitty rolled her eyes in frustration. "Ebony is awake and has already put Vulcan to sleep. If you don't get out here and help me and Lupo . . . well, we're afraid of what she'll do next."

The stables were quiet as horses were finishing their tea. Someone turned the radio on. Burmese chewed the last mouthful of oats and then slipped her head over to the stable latch. In one quick movement she had it unbolted.

"What are we waiting for?" she asked, as the door swung open.

10
Happy Birthday!

The sound of children's laughter floated down the corridors of Buckingham Palace. Holly could hear the whoops and screams of joy coming from the cosy living room. She knew that members of the royal family, along with the palace servants and guards, were all watching as the Queen's birthday cake was presented. As was the custom every year, all the dogs would get a cuddle and a chance to taste the finest cake in the land.

Holly was sad to be missing out. She didn't want to admit it to Lupo but she was also scared. All of a sudden, the palace felt very big. Guarding it and the family would need an army. She hoped Kitty would return with help and that Herbert would rally the mice. "One corgi and a cocker spaniel does not an army make," she said to herself.

Lupo was too busy sniffing for George. He caught the familiar scent of the Prince, and he looked up the wide palace staircase. "Nanny said she was going to take George to the playroom. I think I have him, but it's a very faint trace I am picking up."

Holly ran up the stairs. "Follow me. The playroom is on the third floor. Don't worry, we'll get to him before they do. I know all the speedy routes around this palace and they don't!"

Lupo followed Holly to the top of the grand staircase. He couldn't help but feel just a little bit amazed by the imposing nature of the curved stairs as they made their ascent. Heavy gilt decorations towered over him. Overhead, a magnificent glass dome cast the eclipse's darkened skies down on to the full-length portraits of Queen Victoria and her family.

At the top of the stairs they stood in the middle of a long corridor in which elaborately decorated white and gold doors led to the Queen's private rooms. On the walls were priceless works of art, and vases filled with flowers rested on a series of plinths. Lupo had to resist the urge to jump up on to a red silk sofa.

Holly pushed open the second door on the left. "There's a trap door in the Blue Room that can take us to a staff staircase," she said, then added, "Quick, someone's coming."

Sure enough, Tommy the footman was walking along the corridors, looking for the missing corgi. "Holly! Where are you? Holly, I've got cake for you!" he called out.

The door shut behind them, leaving Tommy whistling outside. The Blue Room took Lupo's breath away. He felt so small compared to the imposing royal portraits that glared down at him. Grand mirrors, silk-covered chairs and more golden carvings bore down on an impressively large rug. Flowers in brilliant pinks and blues littered the floor. Lupo stuck his black nose to the floor, hoping to smell the blooming bouquet.

Holly giggled. "I do that . . . shame that it's only a rug!"

"Where's the trap door, anyway?" Lupo said, attempting to hide his embarrassment. "Of course I knew the flowers weren't real. I just thought I . . ."

The pretty corgi was next to a tall window. "It's behind these curtains. I hope you're feeling strong, because this door rarely gets used any more. PUSH!"

There was a table with some blue vases on top of it. Queen Mary looked down from a large picture with disapproving eyes. Underneath the table was a door. They pushed it open and found a set of narrow stairs. Holly assured him it was the quickest route to the playroom on the third floor.

As they ran up the stairs Lupo's thoughts turned to finding the rattle. He had no idea what it looked like. If Ebony wanted it so badly it had to be pretty important. If it was old, priceless and Egyptian, chances are it had ended up in the British Museum.

Holly had different ideas about where it might be. "I just have a feeling that the rattle never left this palace," she said as she began a second set of stairs. "We're nearly there – one more flight. Bertie's journals said that he gave everything to Queen Victoria and we know she just put the whole lot in the pantry."

Lupo thought that Holly would be right. "That might be, Holly," he said, "but where are we going to look? It could be anywhere here."

Holly smiled sweetly. "Not necessarily. I think I

have a pretty good idea where to start."

The top of the stairs was in sight. Holly used her front left paw to open an exit. They found themselves standing in the middle of a corridor on a plush, navy blue carpet. There were no paintings on display. No vases or flowers. The walls were white and the elaborate gold carvings replaced with simple wood.

"Looks nothing like downstairs," said Lupo.

"No, the palace is highly decorated in the state rooms. The everyday bits of it are really rather modest. But don't be fooled – there are more secrets lurking behind these walls. You would be amazed by what I have found over the years. The playroom is through that door there."

Lupo slipped inside. The first thing that he noticed were the stickers that covered the painted door. A child had clearly spent a great deal of effort decorating it a long time ago. The stickers weren't new. They were old-fashioned pictures of horses cantering in full tack, cats playing with balls of wool, dogs chewing big bones, alongside children in long white nightgowns decorating a bright green Christmas tree.

Fortunately the door was slightly ajar. "The

Queen herself used to play in here. Go in, I'll keep an eye out for anyone."

Lupo nudged the door wider and walked in. Immediately, he spotted Nanny. She was fast asleep. George was playing on the floor, surrounded by hundreds of wooden soldiers.

"Lupo!" he said, bouncing up and down around the wooden army. His soft face beamed as he *gurgled* merrily. "I did it. Nanny took me to the playroom. Look at all the toys!"

Lupo was happy to see that George was unaffected by the day's events. He responded to the Prince by wagging his tail frantically left and right, *chomping* a couple of times and *shaking* his head.

"Well done, buddy," he said. "Look, George, I need you to climb into that toy cart. It's not safe for you to be playing alone up here. There is a very bad cat that is trying to take over the palace."

"Holly, he's OK," he said, looking over to his friend outside the door.

As well as George's soldiers, the playroom was filled with old toys. Children's books, bound in leather and trimmed with gold, lined the big wooden shelves. Teddy bears sat around a small table enjoying a tea party with the very best china. Snakes and Ladders, Monopoly, Scrabble and an old chessboard had been set up on another table. A pair of rocking horses made from fine wood, painted black and wearing official uniform, waited patiently for riders alongside a huge doll's house. But Prince George had eyes only for the little wooden soldiers.

Lupo heard a rustling of feathers and paws coming towards the room. Quickly, he rolled the tiny red cart over to the toddler. It was filled with building blocks. Holly ran in to help, grabbing the knitted blanket off Nanny's lap and draping it over the Prince. George made sure that wombat was carefully tucked in.

"That must be Ebony's followers. We need to get out of here," said Lupo.

Holly ran to the far end of the room. "Through here."

A heron, hippo and elephant burst in moments later. Ebony's followers raided the room, looking for the little Prince – only to eventually leave empty-handed.

"That was close!" said Holly.

"Too close," answered Lupo. "Where do you

think this rattle is? Nanny is already asleep, which must mean that Ebony's powers are getting stronger."

"I don't understand. If Nanny's asleep, why isn't George? He's human. Wouldn't Ebony have put him to sleep too?" asked Holly.

"My guess is that she wanted Prince George for something," answered Lupo. "And I'm not about to let that cat get her claws into him. I wonder how Kitty's getting on? Let's just hope she's gathering a really big army because I think once Ebony is ready she is going to put her curse on Buckingham Palace."

"We need to get to the Egyptian room – it's in the west wing near the Chinese room," said Holly.

Lupo grabbed a skipping rope that had been tossed on the floor near the playroom door. He attached it to the cart and his collar. "An Egyptian room, a Chinese room, old playrooms. Is there anything this palace doesn't have? Ready!"

"Remind me to show you the doggy grooming salon one day. Now that *really* is something! I like to think of it as a spa for dogs," said Holly. She walked out of the room, checking the corridor was clear before signalling to Lupo and George.

* * *

"Ta-daaa!" she barked.

Lupo had never been so lost. Every finely kept room looked the same. They had walked down so many red-carpeted hallways that at times he wondered if he wasn't being walked round and round in circles. Soon they were standing in front of a very old-looking door covered in hieroglyphics.

Holly ran to a small guard's chair near the door. "Help me drag it to the handle. You're taller than me – do you think you can get us in there?"

"These markings are the same as the ones on Bertie's old desk," said Lupo, curious. He untied the skipping rope and helped Holly, although he wasn't sure how Her Majesty would feel about two dogs dragging her furniture around. "What's in there?" he asked as they readied the chair.

Holly was confident. "Wait and see!" She was positively bouncing from paw to paw with glee. "I've only been in here once. I just know it's going to be where we find the rattle. I just *know* it!"

Lupo hopped on to a priceless Georgian antique chair. Then, using his front teeth and his left paw, he managed to turn the elaborate doorknob. They were in.

Immediately, he sniffed the air and detected

something familiar. Beyond the door he could see darkness. The curtains in the room where closed. The air smelt musty and foreign. "Ancient Egypt . . ." he growled softly.

"Yup," began Holly. "Welcome to the eighth Wonder of the World." She pushed the door wider to let in the light from the hallway.

As he pulled the little red cart into the room, George gasped, "*E-pit*, Lupo!"

Lupo felt like they had been transported though time to ancient Egypt. The floors were huge slabs of the finest sandstone. All around him were tall columns. On closer inspection, he saw that they were all marked with strange animal hieroglyphics. He was captivated. In all his adventures around all the other royal palaces he had never been into a room decorated in ancient Egyptian artefacts. He ran a paw over a painting of what looked like a human with a dog's head.

But then his nose twitched. He knew that trouble was close by. He remembered the Duke's story. This room looked *exactly* how he had imagined the cat's burial tomb . . .

"I was up here with the Queen's husband the day

after he found the journals," said Holly. "I watched him do rubbings of that symbol a couple of times. Do you know what it means?"

Lupo felt the hairs on the back of his neck rise as he investigated the symbol, which resembled a dog. "Not a clue, but I don't like that it looks exactly like the markings I saw on the side of the Ebony's sarcophagus. It looks like a big dog, doesn't it?"

George rubbed the marking with his little hand, saying, "Woof!"

"Yes, wait – there's more! Look at this . . ." Holly said, standing in front of a pair of ageing yellow stone dogs in red and gold cloaks. Both were holding sharp spears, their eyes painted white and blue. Lupo noticed more of the same dog statues around the room. Most of them were standing but others were sitting – and all of them appeared to be guarding something. "Holly, I think there was a tomb Bertie discovered but didn't write about."

Holly stood next to what appeared to be a daybed. "It's possible," she said. "Queen Victoria had a passion for all things Egyptian and Asian. She had rooms filled with the things she collected. In here she put all her treasures from the ancient world, such as the finest cottons and silks from the Orient. She used to spend a lot of time in here after her beloved Prince Albert died, talking to herself, apparently." Holly paused, pointing to a big key on a golden tassel behind the door. "The door was always locked, but the guards swore they could hear her talking to someone." She pulled a curtain back to properly reveal the true extent of Victoria's collection.

Prince George climbed out of his cart and started crawling around amongst the precious goblets and trinkets, occasionally picking them up and examining them before dropping them back on the floor. Amongst the artefacts was a desk that seemed to be covered in silvery snakes. Behind it was a chair which looked like it had been carved from the bones of a very large animal. Lupo ran over, jumped up on to the chair and sniffed the goblets.

"People were here recently," he said, jumping off again. "There is still wine in these cups. That's odd." As he moved, he saw that an ancient hand-painted stone had been nailed to the walls. "Look at this, Holly. They're called friezes. They tell a story. See, everything on the walls is a story about the past."

On the picture closest to the door Lupo saw two figures. His heart slowed but he could still feel the blood pumping around his body. He was motionless because what he was looking at made no sense whatsoever.

Holly joined him and was the first to speak. "How can it be?"

Lupo ran to the back of the room so that he could get a better look. Painted on the stone in incredible detail was the story of two creatures – a dog and a cat. There was no doubt it was a spectacular tale. The large black dog and the black cat in the first stone painting were sitting side by side dressed as great rulers. They were wearing what looked like ancient golden uniforms. All around them animals of every size sat or lay in the picture. It was a celebration of creatures.

Lupo was impressed but also suspicious. After stumbling into one tomb today, he was concerned they had just stumbled into another.

"Ebony," said Lupo out loud.

George was beneath the friezes, trying to reach up and grab at the life-sized cat. "Meow!" he said.

Holly was shocked. "Is that what she looks like?

Oh my, we really are in trouble. Please tell me she is not quite so big?"

"No, she isn't," said Lupo. "If that is Ebony, though, then who is the dog? The painting looks to me like it's telling us that at some point they ruled together."

"Lupo!" gurgled Prince George. He stuck his thumb in his mouth, grabbed his wombat and rolled on his back.

"You have to admit," said Holly, stepping towards it to get a better look, "that dog does look a bit like you. George is right."

Lupo turned his attention to the picture in which Ebony was holding high a red stone. The animals all around seemed in awe – except the ruling black dog, which looked sad. In the next image, Ebony was alone on her throne whilst her sphinxes stripped the dog of its power. Its headdress was given to a nasty-looking black cobra.

Lupo gazed at the next picture with particular interest. A wide blue river ran between the dog and Ebony. The black dog was carrying a large spear with Ebony's red stone in the middle of it, which he was aiming *at* Ebony. Behind the cat were three familiar figures: a heron, a hippo and an elephant, all of them looking over to the dog across the river.

Lupo exclaimed, "Holly, the dog took her power! Don't you see? That was what the red stone is – it's the source of her goddess power. The dog took it away."

Holly nodded. "Lupo, you see the strange mark on the red stone he's holding? It looks just like the same stone on Her Majesty's crown. It's called the Black Prince Ruby!"

They turned to the picture where the cat and the dog appeared to be at war. They clashed to great cost and many animals fell. George gurgled as he snuggled up with his wombat. Lupo wished they were back in the safety of the nursery.

The last picture was the brightest of them all. The dog was holding the spear with the ruby high in the sky. The cat was lying beneath him. Egypt seemed calm once again. The animals rejoiced and the humans returned.

Holly perked up. "I know where I've seen that dog before. I might be wrong, but that dog looks a lot like Queen Victoria's dog, Noble. Could it be him?"

Lupo's bright eyes spotted something in the far corner of the first picture. Ebony was holding a strange object.

He said, "I'm not sure, Holly. If today has taught me anything it's to expect the unexpected and nothing would surprise me less than one of Queen Victoria's dogs turning out to be some ancient god-like dog. Look at that," he continued, inspecting the final drawing. "I think we've found the rattle." He made a note of the strange-looking object Ebony was clutching in the last frieze.

"You mean the one Ebony is holding? It looks like an instrument to me, not a rattle at all," remarked Holly.

"That *must* be it," said Lupo. "Now all we need to do is find it."

There were several large chests. Together, they opened the first, and were both surprised to find it full of pale sand. They had a good rummage around but found nothing more. Lupo said, "Now that really is odd. Why would anyone want a box full of sand?"

Holly shrugged her shoulders. "Let's try the second box."

The second box was also full of sand.

They were both baffled. George crawled over and tried to clamber up to investigate too, but Lupo stopped him from climbing in. "George, I don't know what the sand is for but I don't think you should get in. This isn't like the sandpit at Kensington Gardens."

Meanwhile, Holly had managed to open the last one. "Lupo, I think you were right. Bertie *did* stumble on to more than one tomb whilst he was lost in that sandstorm."

At the royal stables things were going exactly as Kitty had planned. Burmese would wait for them in the palace gardens behind some big trees. Matilda told Kitty that it was where she would be able to enjoy a large selection of prize-winning marigolds.

Matilda and Kitty headed for the tunnels that would take them all the way to the City of Creatures. The plan was to spread the word at the Katz Bar that every cat was needed at Buckingham Palace. Kitty watched as Matilda got to work organizing what would be the biggest ever gathering of London cats.

* * *

It had been a long time since Kitty had been so far into the underground sewers and she was shocked to see just how many animals had taken up residence within the dark Victorian tunnels. Unfamiliar faces popped out to check them out as they passed. The residents blinked and snorted, clearly annoyed that the famous palace cat was travelling through their secretive world.

Kitty had often heard Herbert talking to Lupo about crocodiles and huge snakes living in the waterways, so she was automatically on her guard, unlike Matilda who was happiest "amongst her folk". She walked with a confident swagger at every awkward twist and turn, grinning like a Cheshire cat.

Charlotte had never been to MI5 headquarters before. Mice without clearance were not allowed – nor did they dare – to venture this far into Hyde Park. She felt very important walking alongside Herbert.

A group of mice sat watching monitors. Herbert explained that they were "lookout mice". Another group sat at their desks cracking codes and another were deep in calculations and filing detailed reports.

"This place is brilliant!" she said as they arrived at the door to his office.

He opened it for her. "Come in, my dear, come on in."

A junior agent sat with her pen at the ready, willing to take any necessary notes. She was a particularly keen student, which was good since she would be responsible for guarding any future royal princesses. She promptly stepped forward to introduce herself. "Hello, Charlotte, my name is Chloe."

Charlotte was very impressed with Chloe and admired her strong nose.

"Now that the pleasantries are over," said Herbert, "we have some work to do. Chloe, please can you dig out all the files and books we have on Ebony."

Chloe dropped a file on to Herbert's desk. "One step ahead of you, sir. I received word that she was awake whilst you were en route. Kaye checked in earlier, sir, and said that her cover was blown."

Herbert was studying the slim file of notes on his desk.

"WHAT? KAYE IS AN AGENT? MY *FRIEND* KAYE!" said Charlotte in a state of shock.

"Chloe, perhaps you could arrange some warm

156

milk for our guest and a couple of iced buns," said Herbert, looking over his horn-rimmed spectacles.

"In the pot next to you, sir, but no iced buns today – I thought you were trying to cut back?" said ever-prepared Chloe.

Herbert sloshed the warm liquid into a pretty teacup and gave it to Charlotte, thanking his young agent. The stunned mouse took the milk but didn't drink it. She was too flabbergasted – today was turning out to be somewhat shocking. Herbert tried to hide his disappointment at the lack of tasty treats.

Chloe was walking around the room, reviewing her little notepad at the same time. "Sir, as you can see, we are not only watching Ebony. I dispatched word to the palace this morning to keep an eye on Noble as well. I believe his location has not yet been compromised. Hang on—" she said, grabbing the side of a tiny earpiece she wore in her right ear "— scrap that, Lupo and Holly have just found him."

Herbert finished reading the report. He put it down on his desk and sat for a moment deep in contemplation.

Charlotte was breathlessly waiting for more. "I

didn't think today could get much more INSANE."

"According to these files," said Herbert, "Queen Victoria received the cargo from Bertie and had it moved to the pantry within days of receiving it. Our palace mice reported at the time that Victoria seemed spooked by what she found inside some of the boxes." Herbert went over the notes in his mind, as he tried to piece the puzzle together.

"Spooked?" enquired Charlotte.

"Yes, all our records show that she told her man servant to have the boxes 'put away, far away'. She didn't want them anywhere near her. We know she was frightened of cats."

"I know how she felt," said Charlotte, butting in and shuddering. "This Noble character – who is he?"

Chloe answered politely. "That's the easy bit. Noble was a warrior, a protector. We think that after she lost Prince Albert, Queen Victoria felt safer having him around, watching over her. She must have discovered him within the cargo and instead of banishing him she lavished all her love and affection on him. She even gave him his own room at Buckingham Palace. She wanted him to feel like he was home again – we think this is because the Egyptian room at the palace was an exact replica of the palace throne room he once shared with Ebony."

"OK, so I get the dog," said Charlotte, "but I still don't get what's everyone's worried about. There's a black cat running around Buckingham Palace and some ghostly dog. So what? I have to outrun them all the time! Big deal!"

Chloe's eyes darkened. "Charlotte, it's very serious. You see, Ebony wants revenge against the humans. They took her throne. We know that she has already been able to put half the palace to sleep. Nanny is conked out in the playroom! The maids and all the housekeeping staff are nodding off upstairs. As we speak, the kitchen staff are nodding off below-stairs. The only people who *haven't* been affected so far are the royal family. If Ebony manages to put *them* to sleep, then she has the throne. All it takes is one shake of her rattle."

"And what of Noble?" asked Herbert.

"Too soon to tell. As I said, I have only just had word that he is waking up now. I'll get on it immediately."

"Thank you, Chloe. We can't send that terrible

cat back to where she belongs without Noble's help. Charlotte, I need you to find Kaye and—" Herbert broke off, because he could tell that Chloe was receiving a transmission by the way she was frantically waving at him.

"Sir, I'm receiving reports that mice are evacuating Buckingham Palace," she said. "They say there are cats. Hundreds of them heading for the palace with a – *what?*" Chloe looked bewildered. "Please repeat!" She was looking directly at Herbert as she echoed what she'd heard. ". . . with a horse, sir . . . it's *who*? Sir, it's Burmese!"

Lupo couldn't explain it – his nose told him that Ebony was trouble but that Noble wasn't. He put it down to the fact that Noble was also a dog. Bigger and definitely older, but still a dog. Lupo suspected that he was, in fact, the only thing that could help stop Ebony.

"Let me get this straight: that mummy is supposed to be a dog – Queen Victoria's dog – the dog in the pictures?" asked Holly, staring at a large box in front of Lupo.

"Exactly," said Lupo.

"What now?" asked Holly.

Lupo replied, "We need to wake him up."

This box was much less elaborate. There was no gold mask, no jewels and no sphinx guardians protecting it. The box began to shake.

Holly barked, "I don't like this one bit."

Lupo braced himself for whatever was about to happen.

Noble rose up slowly in his sarcophagus and shook his head. He had a thick black coat and wore several pieces of brown and gold leather that acted as armour. Sand poured out of his ears, along with a dead scarab beetle.

He looked directly at Lupo and Holly. "Thank you for waking me up," he said. "*I* am Noble. I am the protector and warrior to Her Majesty Queen Victoria of England and before that I was the guardian of Egypt. That beetle had been living in my ear for a very long time."

As he hopped out of his box Holly moved closer to Lupo, wary of the stranger.

"I am Lupo and this is Holly. You are in Buckingham Palace and the year is 2015. Queen Elizabeth II rules England, and today is her birthday.

We need your help. Ebony is awake, and she has some kind of sphinx army around her. We are trying to evacuate the royal family to safety."

Noble looked down at the ground – he was clearly unhappy. "It cannot be. Ebony can only arise during a total solar eclipse."

Holly bravely stepped forward. "There was an eclipse today."

"This is not good news," replied Noble, reaching into a leather pouch around his leg. "Fortunately, she doesn't have this." In his large paw was the rattle. Seven tiny bells balanced on slim strings bound to a solid gold handle.

Holly's eyes grew wide. "It's so beautiful!"

Noble handed it to Lupo, saying, "Careful, now – that rattle is dangerous."

"How?" enquired Lupo.

"It may be beautiful but it is also very powerful. Ebony can use it to put trances on creatures and send them to sleep," answered Noble.

Lupo wanted to understand how they both came to wake in the first place. Mummies rising from eternal sleep was nothing short of a miracle. He suspected Queen Victoria had had something to do with it. Sniffing around for a clue, he looked into the old wooden box. Inside were mummy bandages and incense. He inhaled more deeply and picked up spices and honey.

Noble watched as Lupo looked around the box. "It's gone, my friend. Gone for good. When they broke open my resting place they took the Spear of Destiny. *That's* why all this is happening. Ebony and I should have slept for many thousands of years unless disturbed by a ruler of great power. He must be *here* – that's how we are all awake once more. The last time it happened was in the presence of Queen Victoria. She was a fair and wise ruler and she respected animals. My role was to protect the family and the palace. When the spear was found in Prince Bertie's possessions I was finally able to put Ebony back to rest. I gave the spear to Victoria to safeguard against any further attacks. I was woken by you, Lupo. *You* must be the guardian of a great king."

All their eyes turned to look at Prince George who was playing with two wooden soldiers he had taken from the playroom.

Holly calmed down. She softened her growls but

continued to stand guard. "The rattle? I have never heard of a cat having a rattle before. What's it all about?" she asked, taking the rattle from Lupo.

Noble bowed. "The rattle is our curse. If it is shaken three times by a worthy king or queen we will return to our slumber. But if it is shaken by Ebony, every human around the world shall fall into a dreamless sleep. Make no mistake – she will exact her revenge on the humans who took her throne."

Holly rushed forwards. "That can't happen!"

"Stopping Ebony won't be easy," answered Noble humbly.

"No, I didn't think it would be, but fortunately I have a few friends who right about now should be on their way to help us get Ebony back to where she belongs," offered Lupo encouragingly.

Noble said, "Good. Come now – all we need is my spear. It's the only way to stop her." He put the pretty rattle back in his pouch and headed for the door.

Herbert heard about the cats advancing towards Buckingham Palace and ran as fast as his little legs would carry him through the sewers. Cats of every size, shape and colour were gathering in enormous numbers.

Before he left MI5 HQ he instructed Chloe to alert all the Buckingham Palace mice that they were about to be invaded. Mice he could control, but cats were another matter. He understood the logic in getting them *in* – he was just concerned about how he would get them all *out* once the family had fled.

There was another nagging concern. No one had thought to question how Ebony would react to the army of cats headed her way.

11
A Cake Good Enough for a . . . Horse

Vulcan lay awake, trembling at Ebony's paws. He hadn't recovered from being put to sleep. She was far more powerful than even he'd dare believe – and she wasn't about to be told what to do by him. He would have to think hard to come up with a plan to turn things back in his favour.

As Ebony's group of ancient animals finished their preparations for her official coronation, Vulcan stepped forward, bowing lowly.

"Your Majesty," he started. Ebony's green eyes shimmered as he spoke. "You are in a palace. Surely you would like to inspect it? Perhaps I may be so bold as to offer my services? I can give you a guided tour. This room is certainly no home for a cat of your stature. This building has many better, even a throne room – which would be more appropriate for a Queen, Your Majesty?" He could see he had her attention.

"Tell me about Lupo," ordered Ebony. "He is not what I would describe as a royal dog. I looked into your mind and I can see you agree with me. Perhaps you and I have a few things in common, Vulcan?" She continued, "I woke you because I need you. If you give me what I need then I will keep you in my service. I may even give you your own palace. I know how much you want to be a king," she purred.

"Yes, Your Highness," replied Vulcan, hiding his fear at being commanded by a cat. "I would like nothing more than to see Lupo gone. I will serve you well."

"I am going to destroy Lupo for you, Vulcan," said Ebony, sounding especially menacing. "I won't have a dog like him roaming around in my kingdom. He is a pest. He is too loyal to the humans. The animals around here like him too much. I plan on crushing him like a bug!"

Vulcan smiled crookedly, showing off his old grey teeth.

"I have sent my cobra to find him," she said.

"Take me to the Throne Room, Vulcan. Then I will consider how you will best fit into my new kingdom."

Vulcan noticed that the ancient Queen seemed to be gaining strength. All afternoon she had been changing: her black fur had grown thicker and her eyes had turned a brighter shade of green.

"My powers have almost completely regenerated," she said. "It is time I took my throne and began to rule this nation." She walked elegantly out of the pantry and into Buckingham Palace. Behind her the sphinxes followed, each carrying a chest full of sand.

Burmese could hear the stable boys and girls shouting her name; they had obviously noticed she was out of her stable. She longed for the days when she was given a triple-sized stable, fresh soft hay to roll in and only the sweetest carrots.

Matilda found her rolling over and over in the newly-mown grass alongside the tunnel's entrance. "Old friend, we have work to do. Stop messing around."

"This is blissful. I'm never going back to my stable. EVER!" she said, pulling a huge clump of grass out of the Buckingham Palace lawn. A steady stream of cats started to pour out of the tunnel and file into ranks.

Burmese looked toward a group of younger felines. "Is that Nina? Oscar? And little Inky?"

The minute the young cats saw Burmese they ran over to play with the old royal charger. "Burmese!" they meowed. "It's good to see you!"

Matilda put a stop to all the fun and games. "Burmese, stop swinging those cats around. If Kitty sees you mucking around she'll be . . ."

Just then, Kitty emerged from the tunnel. She had never felt more dirty. "Yuck, it's really horrible down there. Right, you lot, get yourselves into some kind of order – young cats at the back and let's have old cats at the front."

One hundred, two hundred, two hundred and fifty cats – and counting – were now massed in smart rows on the palace lawn.

"They can't hear you," neighed Burmese. "Hold on!" And with that, she picked Kitty up with her teeth and swung the tabby on to her back.

Every cat fell silent. Kitty was ready to be heard.

The heir to the throne, the Prince of Wales, was the

first to notice something odd happening in the garden. He stopped eating the birthday cake he'd been given and walked towards the windows.

"Has anyone else noticed that there seems to be rather a lot of CATS on the lawn?"

His wife, the Duchess, laughed loudly, "CATS?"

"Mummy," said the Prince to his mother, the Queen, "I think you might want to see this. There is a CAT meowing on Burmese's back and, Mummy, there appears to be an army of cats listening to it!"

Lupo jumped down from the window ledge. "They have arrived and it looks like Kitty has brought us an army!"

Holly and Noble ran towards the Banqueting Hall. With the rattle safely tucked away in his pouch, Noble was confident he would be able to get Ebony back to sleep. Lupo raced ahead, pulling George along in the little red cart.

"FASTER, LUPO!" the young Prince cried as they raced down the Queen's gallery.

As he turned at the elbow of the corridor on his way to the living room, they were forced to a complete stop. Ebony was blocking the path. Surrounded by

her guardians, she stood tall on the back of a large crocodile. The heron seemed to be taking notes on a long scroll. The hippo snapped its jaws open and closed, showing off an impressively large set of teeth. Behind them, the cobra slithered, hissing loudly.

"We're too late – her powers have completely regenerated," said Noble.

Holly joined Lupo beside the little red cart, protecting Prince George. "Oh no, he's right, Lupo. What are we going to do?"

"LUPO . . ." purred Ebony. "Bring me the rattle and Prince George."

Vulcan pushed his way in front. This he had to see.

Lupo stood his ground against the black cat. He growled back. "NEVER. YOU WILL NOT HURT MY FAMILY!"

"I see you have found Noble," sneered Ebony.

Noble spoke solemnly and clearly. "This is not your time, Ebony. You must not hurt these innocent animals. They are trying to protect their humans. You will not win this fight and you will return to your eternal sleep."

"I won't let you take Prince George," Lupo added

173

confidently. "You will have to come through me first."

"Poor little puppy. You see, I don't want to just get my revenge. I mean to rule," said Ebony. "NOW, BRING ME THE PRINCE!"

Noble stepped back so he too was protecting the young prince. Ebony rode her crocodile towards them. It was so close that Lupo could smell the scaly creature's fishy breath.

"You think you are so powerful – Noble, the Guardian of Egypt," Ebony mocked. "I notice you have no Spear of Destiny. How exactly are you going to stop me?" she probed.

Noble stood perfectly still, with Lupo by his side, and said, "Return to your resting place or I shall force you back."

Ebony replied, "Noble, you are a fool. You shall not stop me. At this very moment I am gathering a great army of cats. One look at me and they will do whatever I want. You'll see. HISS! Grab LUPO!"

A thunderous roar and gust of wind cascaded all around them. Lupo grabbed on to the little red cart. Holly clung on to Noble, all of them huddling as close together as they could in the swirling storm.

"HOLD ON TO ME," he said.

The corridor filled with sand. It poured out of several chests that looked different to those that Lupo and Holly had found in the Egyptian room. It flew around them, forcing them back into a doorway to take cover. Prince George was hiding under his little blanket with wombat. When the sand subsided, Ebony had gone, along with Vulcan and her guardian mob. Only the cobra remained. It whipped its tail in the fine sand that now lay on the carpet.

"HISS!" it said as it inched it way closer to Lupo. "One bite and you will sleep for ever. HISS!"

Holly let go of Lupo and Noble. "We are in serious trouble. That cobra isn't going away and worse, our plan has backfired. Ebony is going to turn Kitty's army to her advantage."

Lupo shook his head. "What have I *done?*" he said.

The yellow silk curtains fluttered in the madness as a sandstorm filled the room. Palace guards rushed in, attempting to rescue the family from the whirlwind around them. George's uncle tried to stop the mighty Burmese from crashing through the living room doors. But it was no good. One by one the royal family disappeared amongst a tornado of sand.

The cobra forced Lupo, Noble and Holly into the room. The little red cart was swept up into the sand. Prince George waved merrily as the cart whizzed around in the incredible winds, meowing excitedly as he watched hundreds of cats swarming into the palace living room from the gardens.

The guards tried to force the cats back, only to get sucked into the twirling sand. Two sphinxes appeared and grabbed Noble's pouch. He fought back but it was no good.

"THE RATTLE!" was the last thing Noble said before the sphinxes carried him into the eye of the tornado.

Kitty jumped off Burmese's back, landing on a bookcase. The storm was now accelerating in the Queen's living room. The carpet was being torn up. A shredded sofa was sucked clean into the winds and then promptly spat out.

Lupo took cover behind a curtain, holding on to Holly as she flew high into the air. He wrapped a curtain-tie around his waist and then slung it around her so that they were together.

As quickly as it had arrived, the storm was gone. All that remained in the royal living room was upturned furniture and torn-up floorboards. Only one cat was left.

Burmese was busy tucking into the Queen's very impressive birthday cake, unaware anything abnormal had happened at all.

Herbert leapt through the double doors into the room. "Is everyone all right?"

Kitty jumped down from the bookcase. "I think so. What just happened?"

Lupo sniffed the air. "Ebony has turned Kitty's army of cats against us. And worst of all, she has the royal family."

"Where have they gone?" Holly asked desperately.

Lupo sniffed the floor and scratched the floorboards. "They're still in the palace. I can smell them."

Herbert looked around. The living room was filled with sand. Party balloons bobbed around listlessly in the corner. Burmese had moved on to the second tier of Her Majesty's birthday cake. Willow, the Queen's corgi, crawled out from under a grand piano. She dusted herself off, and looked around the horror, unsure of which disaster to approach first. Behind her the Queen's dorgi, Candy, looked to see if the coast was clear. They'd had a lucky escape.

Willow shook the sand from her coat, and said, "Holly, what on earth is Lupo doing here? And who on earth was that dog you were with? If I find out any of you have anything to do with this I will have your heads on dinner plates! Candy, you can come out now. Hurry up! Out!"

Willow continued, "Herbert, I don't know what's going on – and I am sure there is a good explanation . . . One minute we are all enjoying a very pleasant chorus of 'Happy Birthday' and the next there's a hundred dirty cats, a sandstorm and Burmese in the middle of the yellow drawing room. Just look at the mess! Burmese is eating Her Majesty's birthday cake! This will not do!"

Candy barked in agreement.

Monty was fast asleep and snoring on the Duke of Edinburgh's armchair, where he had been all afternoon. The entire event had completely passed over him.

Lupo wasn't listening. He went to the corner of the room where Noble had been taken. He examined the sand and said, "Ebony has them and Noble too."

Kitty brushed sand out of her eyes and rubbed her fur against the side of an upturned yellow chintz sofa. "The entire royal family is now under her spell. They have suffered the curse! This is exactly what I was afraid of."

Willow demanded to know what that meant.

Lupo stepped in to explain. "Every human in this palace is lost in a deep sleep. They shall not wake unless the curse is lifted. We need to find Noble's spear. He told us that it's the only way to stop Ebony and get the family back."

Holly howled long and hard. Finally, when she felt she could speak she said. "I will not rest until my family is safe. This cat is going to bed if it's the last thing I do!"

12
Lights Out

Lupo ushered everyone in a circle in the living room. "We need to stick together. That's the first thing. Now, Willow, have you seen an ancient spear? It's called the Spear of Destiny. Has the Queen got it?"

Candy was still shaking as she spoke. "The Queen has a spear which is very old. It's in her study. She once had a scientist from the British Museum look at it and he confirmed it was most likely ancient Egyptian, but of little value. Queen Victoria apparently slept with it under her bed. I believe it was given to her by Bertie. Our Queen uses it as a fire poker these days."

"Candy, that's good. That *has* to be it. Once we have it we will need to somehow get it to Noble." He was determined to return Prince George to safety – and fast.

Herbert stuck his hand up. "We have another problem." He pulled a piece of folded paper out of his cardigan pocket, and handed it to Lupo, who opened it out.

QUEEN TO THANK A GRATEFUL NATION WITH BALCONY WAVE

Willow chimed in. "I think I can help with that one. You said that the family is in the building, Lupo?"

"Yes, I can smell them," he answered.

"So it's true, cocker spaniels do have remarkably sensitive noses." Willow smiled. "Well, I am used to balcony appearances. This should be a doddle."

Holly was unsure. "Willow, how exactly are you planning on getting Her Majesty out on to the balcony if she is asleep?"

Willow winked knowingly. "It's all about the smile and the wave, dear."

Lupo and Holly, Kitty and Herbert, Willow and Candy all put their paws together and agreed to get to work. Meanwhile, Monty snorted loudly from his armchair.

Burmese was just getting stuck into the third tier of the birthday cake when Willow snatched it out of her mouth, and shouted, "Pull yourself together! I need you. Your country needs you! This isn't the time for CAKE!"

Lupo tried to lighten the mood as they walked through the deserted palace to the Queen's private study. "Put it this way, everyone," he said. "It's not every day a cat takes over the throne and two horses, one dorgi, corgis, a cocker spaniel, a tabby cat and a mouse get to save the day."

Burmese was impressed with the decorations. Candy told her that she was the only horse that had ever walked the hallowed hallways. When at last they came to the study door they were shocked to find it open with two palace guards fast asleep in a heap on the floor beside it.

Holly grew tense. "That's not right. That door is always closed," she whispered into Lupo's long black ear.

Lupo took a deep breath and walked in, his friends

following closely behind.

"I was wondering where you were hiding," hissed Ebony's cobra. He set his sights on Lupo. "My Queen will be pleased. The Spear of Destiny *and* all the royal pets."

Vulcan was near the fireplace with a poker in his mouth.

Willow was horrified. "Vulcan, you traitor!" she scolded.

Lupo could only watch as all his friends were grabbed by Ebony's army of London cats and sphinxes. Burmese reared up on her hind legs, trying to put up a fight. But it was no good: a whirlwind of sand collected them all from the study. Lupo was left with Hiss. The cobra lunged forward and in one quick move had bitten him. The last thing Lupo heard was Vulcan saying, "Lights out, Lupo. Nighty night. *HISS!*"

Ebony was satisfied with the throne room. She found the cushions very comfortable. Kitty, Herbert and the Queen's dogs looked on. A pair of sleepy footmen served Ebony fresh trout, salmon, prawns and caviar from a silver platter.

One of Ebony's sphinxes bowed. "It is done," he said. "The royal family are all asleep."

Just then, Lupo woke with a sore paw. Hiss's bite had left two small puncture marks in his leg. He barked, hoping to get the footmen's attention but it was no good. Both of them were fast asleep.

"Good job, Hiss," laughed Ebony. "Look at poor Noble sitting in the corner as I take over the world!" She walked over to Noble, who was awake. "Here, boy, fetch!" she said, laughing and waving the spear in the air.

Noble stared into Ebony's green eyes. "That spear is useless in anyone's paws but mine."

"Perhaps," said Ebony. She walked back to her prisoners. "BRING IN THE CATS!"

Kitty watched as Ebony's army entered the throne room and sat, waiting for their orders.

Ebony meowed. "You see, my work here is already complete. The human Queen Elizabeth sleeps soundly and I am here to restore balance. Cats will be treated with the respect they deserve!"

Lupo whispered loudly so that all

his friends could hear. "They are asleep! The entire army of cats is under a spell. Look at their eyes!"

Every cat had its eyes half shut. As the cats took their places, they dragged their paws as if they were walking in a dream.

In amongst the cat army, Matilda was waking. She felt very dizzy. The entire room seemed to be moving. A spell, she thought. That's what she did – she put us all under some kind of ancient spell.

Ebony was covered in a golden coat. On top of her head was the Imperial State Crown. "I HAVE THE BLACK PRINCE RUBY! I AM QUEEN!" she declared from the red throne.

Matilda was powerless to do anything. All her friends were sitting in the same position, paws outstretched, lying flat on their bellies. Not a single cat moved a muscle as they listened to the mighty Ebony. In the far corner she heard Lupo growling.

"Let us begin. You will be my loyal guards. I want you on duty throughout the palace and the city. No one gets in or out of here. Understood?"

Every cat meowed at the same time. Matilda watched with astonishment but played along, as if she too was still in the trance.

"Tonight we feast my victory. Tomorrow we take the world!" Ebony said, waving her golden rattle high in the air. By now it was obvious that it was the source of all her power. Matilda watched as Ebony stroked it, like it was a loving pet.

All the cats were being given a golden collar. Matilda received hers from Ebony personally. As Ebony clipped Matilda's collar into place the old grey cat groaned at the weight of it. Fortunately, Ebony failed to notice. Matilda was determined to play along until she got the opportunity to snatch back the rattle. That wouldn't be easy for some cats, but Matilda knew exactly how to "fake being under Ebony's spell".

"Take the prisoners out of here. And lock them up with the young prince," commanded Ebony.

Once again, Lupo felt the lights go out, even though he was far from ready to go to bed.

13
A Royal Wave

Lupo opened his eyes. On the bed above him Prince George was *gurgling* away. "Wake up, Lupo!"

Not wanting to waste a single second, Lupo jumped on to the bed to see if George was OK. He wasn't surprised to find the toddler in good spirits and delighted to see his pal. Waving his hands around, he said, "Wake up," to Herbert and then to Kitty.

One by one, everyone stirred. Noble was the last to wake and he was very happy to see the toddler.

Herbert studied the little prince. Rubbing his whiskers, he mused, "How is it that George is awake? How come he's unaffected by the curse – and how did he wake *us* up?"

"The curse will not affect someone so young.

He will be a fine King someday. Like Queen Victoria before him, he loves animals," said Noble. "His love alone is strong enough to break the spell on us. My King!" Noble bowed to the toddler, who was trying to catch Herbert.

Lupo saw they were in a pale green and gold bedroom, its floor covered in sand. "Noble, if George was able to wake us up, can't he wake the rest of the palace?"

Noble was smiling at the young child. "No, unfortunately not. For that, Prince George would need the rattle. Once he has it he can wake the humans and lift the curse."

Holly heard noises and went to the bedroom window. A large crowd had gathered outside Buckingham Palace. They had come to see their Queen. Holly looked at a digital clock on the bedside table.

"It's time for the WAVE!" she cried. "Quick, we have to get the Queen on to the balcony and fast!"

Willow grabbed Burmese who was enjoying munching on some Murray mints that had been left in a fine china bowl by the door.

"Eating again? *Really?*" said Willow to the

chocolate-brown horse. "Burmese, you need to take us all to the Queen. Get on Burmese's back, everyone."

"Climb on, but no one pull on my ears. I can't stand it when my ears get pulled. I'm frightfully ticklish!"

Lupo took a running jump and landed on Burmese's back, giving her a fright. "Her Majesty will be asleep in her bedchamber. We don't have much time, Willow. I hope you have a good plan!"

Burmese stopped eating. She picked Prince George up with her teeth and plonked the wriggling toddler on to her back. The Prince was a natural rider.

"Rocking horse!" he said as he *squirmed* and *burbled* happily on the horse's back.

Lupo *chomped* into his ear. "Hold on tight!"

"Burmese, straight out the door and it's the third door on the left! Hurry!" said Willow.

With everyone on board, Burmese bolted out of the door. The cat guards ran for cover as the Queen's prized horse charged down the corridor in the direction of the royal bedchamber. There were no guards at the door when they arrived. Herbert ran down the horse's face and turned the doorknob.

Lupo was the first to spot the Queen. "Look, over there! Burmese – the bed!" he said.

Willow landed on the bed with a thud. Burmese carefully assisted the young Prince on to the Queen's peach-coloured quilted blanket.

Kitty was in a state of shock. "Look at her. She looks like she is wide awake . . ."

The Queen was dressed in her finest royal state robes over a pretty white dress. But Her Majesty was blissfully unaware that standing in her bedroom was her horse, several dogs, a mouse and a tabby cat.

"Get her sunglasses – they're in the top drawer. And be quick!" barked Willow to Candy.

Candy knew exactly where all the Queen's accessories were kept.

"Well done, Candy!" said Willow. "Right, everyone! We need to get her on to Burmese's back."

Down on the ground, children waved their flags and photographers snapped away as the doors to the balcony finally opened. Gasps of approval, together with a huge cheer, rippled through the crowd as the great British public looked at their Queen in all her glory.

Queen Elizabeth II rode on to the balcony at Buckingham Palace on the back of her favourite horse wearing a very big pair of round horseracing sunglasses and her Robes of State. The crowd roared, eagerly awaiting her wave.

Underneath the thick velvet cape, Lupo was struggling to hold on. He was under the Queen's left arm and Kitty was beneath her right. Together they were keeping the Queen balanced. "Hang on, everyone, nearly there! We just need the wave – Herbert, quick!"

Burmese felt like she was back at Horse Guards Parade. She loved the big crowd. "They're taking my picture!" she neighed with glee.

Thousands of people cheered for their monarch. Herbert didn't want to let them down. He ran down her arm and ducked into the sleeve of her white dress. Running along her arm he stopped at her hand. "READY!" he said as Lupo pushed her arm high into the air.

"This is it!" Lupo warned everyone.

Willow was trying her best to keep Her Majesty upright. "I'm not sure how much longer I can hold her up!"

Herbert starfished his little body against the back of her hand and pulled it up with all his might. "NOW!"

The Queen, asleep on the back of her horse, waved to her grateful public, with a little help from Herbert, Lupo, Holly, Kitty and Prince George.

The crowds swelled and cheered with delight. Burmese blew a kiss to all the people below.

"CAN WE PLEASE GET OUT OF HERE!" said Kitty, desperately trying to keep the Queen on her feet.

Only when they were back behind closed doors did everyone breathe a deep sigh of relief.

The Queen was now propped up in a chair. Prince George had loved every minute of his first trip out on to the balcony, even if it was underneath the Robes of State. He crawled closer to Lupo *gurgling*, "More waving, more!"

Lupo sniffed into his ear and licked the side of George's face. "That was too close, George. I don't think we can do it again. Nice one, everyone," he said, knowing that their troubles were far from over.

14
Cats Rule!

In the banqueting hall, the palace chefs cooked under Ebony's spell. They prepared the feast just as they would for any other state occasion, only they were cooking whilst being fast asleep. On the menu was fresh fish and poached chicken, followed by a creamy Scottish salmon mousse. Ebony's army was in cat heaven.

Meanwhile, at the other end of the table, Vulcan was growing more uncomfortable. He noticed that Ebony was terribly vain. At every mirror she passed, she would stop and lovingly gaze at herself.

"I am the prettiest Queen of them all!" she purred.

But the cat Queen was no match for the human monarch. She wore many fine jewels, it was true. Vulcan relished the sight of them and wondered just how much loyalty a single diamond would buy him. All down Ebony's paws were many golden bangles. Around her middle she wore what looked like a skirt, only it was made entirely from pieces of gold, individually crafted to look like ostrich feathers. She was wearing the Imperial State Crown, claiming that the Black Prince Ruby looked much better now that it was set into a crown. The crown was too big, however, so it shifted from side to side as she tried to walk and talk at the same time.

Around the banqueting table sat many of her heads of state, including the ancient elephant, hippo and heron. Vulcan saw that they were counselling her on her plans for her new animal palace. If she got her way, Buckingham Palace would look very different.

Tommy the footman put a plate of salmon in front of Vulcan. Instantly, Vulcan felt his tummy turn over. Fish was not his thing. Worst of all, Ebony had barely spoken to him. She gave just the slightest bit of attention when she wanted something – unlike Queen Elizabeth who would lavish treats and cuddles on him whenever he went near. It was safe to say that this was not what he had had in mind when he switched sides.

Hiss sidled up to him and said, "Vulcan, you aren't eating, *hiss*, not hungry? The food too rich for you, *hiss*?" Vulcan pushed the plate away. Hiss wrapped himself around Vulcan's chair. "Never mind. I suspect we shall be done with you soon now that we have the Spear of Destiny, *hiss*."

Vulcan smiled to himself. He knew that Ebony was clinging on to an ordinary brass poker. The real spear was safely tucked away. His time was coming.

The ancient cat queen climbed up on to the back of a large elephant and began her speech.

"Welcome, my fellow cats. Soon we will begin turning this house into a palace fit for a ruler such as myself. You will all be given homes within my new domain. Fear not, you shall never have to go back to the underworld that is the CITY OF CREATURES. It is time for the humans to feel what is like to live in darkness. Soon they will all be banished to the blackness!"

Vulcan felt his heart pound in his chest.

"Tomorrow, I shall send the nation into a deep sleep. Using this!" Ebony lifted the golden rattle in the air. "It will take all my strength!"

Vulcan raised an eyebrow. This was getting

interesting. Ebony continued to preach to her masses. "CATS WILL RULE. Repeat as loudly as you can . . ."

The cats meowed in response:

"CATS RULE!"

"CATS RULE!"

"CATS RULE!"

Vulcan's gaze landed on one old grey cat at the end of the room. It was sitting next to the elephant, and it was the only feline not to obey the mighty Ebony. Vulcan knew he had finally found the chink in Ebony's army. The one cat who was awake and who was not going to follow a single order it was given – Matilda.

Lupo could hear the cats meowing from as far away as the balcony. They had been too busy with their feasting to notice the crowds of humans outside the palace windows.

Kitty heard it too. "I wonder if Matilda is all right," she said to him. "She can take care of herself. I just hope that she doesn't do anything stupid. That Ebony is more dangerous than any of us ever imagined. I grew up believing that she was a force for good, only to find out that she is a crazy, power-hungry creature who will hurt anything that gets in her way. How are you going to stop her, Lupo?"

Lupo comforted his friend by rubbing her shoulder. "Kitty, we *will* get through this. You watch. Sometimes you just have to have a little faith."

Then something happened. Herbert felt the vibrations first. They were stony footsteps and they were headed straight for them. "Something's coming!" he squeaked.

Willow, Holly, Kitty and Burmese hid behind a set of large double doors. Herbert, Candy and Noble helped put Prince George back into the little red cart, which had been left alone near the throne room. The little Prince clung on to his wombat's neck, mumbling, "This is the best great-granny birthday ever! Lots of rides!"

The dogs snuck under a table just in time. A group of sphinxes walked down the corridor. They stopped at Her Majesty the Queen who was slumped lopsided and snoring happily in an armchair.

"What's she doing here?" one said to the other.

"Better get her back where she belongs before Ebony finds out."

Burmese's tail was sticking out of the curtains. Lupo hoped none of the ancient thugs would see it. He watched as they carried the Queen back to her bedchamber.

The noise coming from downstairs was getting louder. Lupo could hear music. George began to bounce around in his cart. He *gurgled*, "Music, Lupo, music!"

They made their way down the stairs and to the door. Burmese gently nuzzled it open, just wide enough for Lupo to squeeze his face through and peer in to the hall. A strong smell of fish and cats hit his senses. He pushed his head further in and saw that Ebony, seated in a chair of pure gold at the far end of the room, was bringing her feast to an end with a dramatic display. All around her cats were dancing and drinking, singing and laughing. Golden harps were plucked by Ebony's sphinxes, and goblets were filled by palace footmen who walked as if in a trance, refilling the cats' cups with warm jugs of honey and milk.

Lupo pulled his face back around to look at all his friends. "Noble, she is at the end of the room. I think she has the rattle. Can you see it?"

It was Noble's turn to look into the room. When he looked back he shook his head. "She has the rattle but not the spear. She seems to be holding on to something else."

Willow pushed past the ancient dog and the cocker spaniel. "Here, let me have a look . . . you're right – she's holding a poker from the fireplace and not the spear at all!"

Lupo knew instantly that Vulcan must have double-crossed Ebony. As Willow described the poker to everyone, Lupo scanned the room for Vulcan. "Vulcan's in there, all right," he said, "but he's not alone. He's talking to an old grey cat."

Kitty popped her head around the door. "AUNTIE MATILDA! She's awake!"

Prince George *groaned*. "Hungry!"

"We need to get him some of that milk. Kitty, can you blend in and get him a goblet?" asked Lupo. "You'll have to be careful."

They all held their breath as she snuck in and tried to grab a full cup off the table but just as she got to the door with it, Ebony stopped the music and the dancing.

"It is time you all took your oath. I shall grant one

of you the ultimate gift. You will live for ever!"

Kitty looked scared. There was no way she could escape. The gang of palace animals watched in silence as she joined the long line leading around the room to Ebony's throne. Each cat received a single gold token.

From the door to the banqueting hall, Lupo could see that Kitty was fidgeting nervously. He could also see that Matilda had spotted Kitty. The old grey cat winked knowingly at Vulcan. The villainous corgi moved into the shadows so that no one but Lupo could see his eyes glimmer. Kitty's aunt then pushed her way down the line so that she was directly behind Kitty.

Lupo held his breath as the long line snaked its way closer to Ebony's throne.

Every cat bowed as it received a treasured token that might be lucky enough to grant them eternal life.

Prince George, Burmese and Herbert all poked their heads into the room to see what was happening at the very same moment Kitty reached the front of the line. No one moved a muscle for fear that the palace tabby would be discovered.

Ebony handed Kitty her token. Kitty tried hard to look anywhere but in the ancient Queen's eyes.

But Ebony stopped, as if she recognized Kitty.

Lupo was about to burst into the room to protect his friend when Matilda flung herself at Ebony, wailing her appreciation. "You have done so much for us! Praise be to Ebony, Queen of these fair feline isles!"

Ebony was initially shocked, then slowly, she accepted the praise. Matilda continued to fawn all over the vain black cat. "She is so beautiful. We are so lucky to have such a special ruler!"

More cats pushed forwards and joined Matilda. Ebony was covered in cats who fell about her, praising the ancient cat's wondrous beauty.

Hiss and the rest of the council watched, satisfied that the throng was under control. They allowed every cat its chance to stumble forwards, and Ebony was lifted high in the air.

Kitty reached up and grabbed the rattle from Ebony's feathered skirt. The ancient cat didn't notice. She was too busy surfing the cats below her.

15
A Present for George

Kitty inched her way through the crowd until she was safely under the table. Then she ran as fast as she could towards Lupo, clutching the golden rattle.

At that moment, Ebony must have discovered her rattle was missing because the room suddenly stopped moving. She dropped to the floor and said, "Who has it? Give it back to me!" None of the cats moved. "Amongst you is a traitor who means to harm your Queen! Find the one amongst you who has deceived me!" she ordered her troops.

Kitty was just centimetres from the door, but Vulcan was blocking her path to freedom. "Give the rattle to me," he snarled at the palace tabby.

Kitty recoiled. "Never!"

As the cats began frantically searching for the

missing rattle, Lupo pushed his way into the room. "ENOUGH!" he barked.

Prince George, riding along in his cart, blew a big bubble and giggled at the sight of the mass of animals.

Vulcan turned to face Lupo, with Willow, Candy and Holly standing directly behind him.

Just then, Herbert ran in and grabbed the rattle from Kitty. He handed it to Lupo.

Lupo lifted it to Prince George, *sniffing* and *growling*. George immediately understood what needed to be done. The little Prince took the rattle and held it tightly.

"ONE SHAKE AND IT IS ALL OVER, EBONY!" warned Lupo.

Ebony laughed. "But he is just a baby. Only a King can wield the power of the rattle. Not some Prince, you foolish dog." She tried to summon up a storm of sand but for some reason her powers refused to work. "I don't understand," she said, bewildered and unsure of herself.

Noble said confidently, "You have no power in the presence of a King. The rattle belongs to the baby, Prince George. He will be the greatest King of them all. He may be young but already he is very powerful. Now, you shall be returned to your eternal sleep."

"NEVER!" cried the frightened black cat. "GET THEM!"

The heron, hippo and elephant all shrank back, ignoring her fearful pleas. They didn't want to be returned to their eternal beds.

"Now, George!" barked Lupo.

George shook the rattle as hard and for as long as he possibly could.

The City of Creatures' cats awoke from their strange trance. Ebony staggered to the back of the hall, taking cover behind her many sphinxes. Matilda jumped on to the table and spoke. "Don't be afraid, city cats! You are in Buckingham Palace. You have been in some kind of trance. Take the food, drink the last of the milk and honey and then return to your homes. Our work here is done."

Ebony whined, "You can't do this. I will return and I will bring with it a far greater curse and an even bigger army. Vulcan – stop that cocker spaniel!"

Vulcan had heard enough. He left the room, only to return moments later carrying Noble's Spear.

"The Spear!" hissed the cobra.

In a last chance to try and regain control, Vulcan aimed the spear at Lupo. "Give me the rattle or I will use the Spear of Destiny."

Lupo lunged forwards, narrowly missing the spear made of gold and wood. Vulcan tried to attack again. This time, he landed a heavy blow. Kitty fell to the ground, listless and still.

Holly charged forwards with Burmese and George's little cart, knocking the spear out of Vulcan's paws.

As Kitty lay injured, the dorgi fled, knowing that his chance was gone. Willow ran after him, crying, "VULCAN, WAIT!"

Noble and Lupo rushed to Kitty's side. Prince George *meowed,* "Kitty! Wake up."

Lupo scooped up the lifeless cat and remembering something said, "Wait . . . just wait . . . any minute."

Ebony's emerald eyes narrowed. In Kitty's palm was the gold token. "It can't be. That's not possible." The black cat was furious.

Kitty's tail moved, then her front paw. Prince George wriggled excitedly. Kitty's ear twitched. One pale green eye opened, then the other. She was awake.

Burmese stuck out her big wet tongue and gave Kitty a big lick. "Rise and shine, Kitty!"

"Is that salmon mousse I can smell?" she asked, and everyone began to laugh.

Noble picked up what remained of the broken spear. Lupo studied it and asked, gently, "Can it be fixed?"

"No, but perhaps it is for the best," said Noble. "We have all been asleep for a long while. Maybe it's time we left the confines of our eternal sleep and joined the world again. It seems to me that you dogs have a pretty good life nowadays and if Kitty was able to find a home for herself perhaps Ebony can too."

Ebony was not amused. "I can't be an ordinary cat. That is ridiculous. I am a queen. I demand you return me to my resting place so I can rise again!"

"No can do," said Noble. "The Spear of Destiny is broken and with it all the power I have is gone. We will have to get used to our new lives in this time."

"I don't want to live in the present!" screeched Ebony.

Noble felt sorry for Ebony, because she had forgotten what it was like to roam free. "Freedom lies in the present. Ebony, you have the world to explore, and to learn from and to enjoy. Let's leave this place and find a new beginning."

Ebony began to cry. "When is the next eclipse?" she pleaded. "Maybe my powers will be restored. Perhaps the gods will take pity on me. At least I have my council." But as she stood there, the council, sphinxes, Hiss and all her golden treasures turned to sand.

Herbert and Matilda managed to escort many of the cats from the palace and back into the tunnels. As they trooped out it was hard for any of them not to notice the damage they were leaving behind.

Herbert, Noble, Willow, Kitty and Candy stood and surveyed the messy trail of broken furniture, shredded carpets and sand scattered throughout the palace.

"We can't wake them up yet." Holly said looking at Prince George with his rattle. "If they see this, we'll all be thrown out of the palace."

"I may not have a rattle, but I do have a few friends who might be able to help us," said Herbert, tapping the floorboards beneath their paws.

Noble chuckled as a tidal wave of palace mice

erupted from every nock and cranny. Herbert oversaw the transformation. They moved like fish in the ocean, scooping up torn carpets and sewing them back together. A side table that was upside down was quickly put upright. The green sofa was plumped up and every grain of sand was hastily removed. The Imperial State crown was returned to its case.

In the banqueting hall, sleeping servants were cleaned up and set out at their posts like rag dolls on the floor. The table was completely cleared and cleaned. One mouse even spent five minutes spraying the room with a neutralizer so that the pong of cats and fish disappeared. Within minutes the whole room was as it should be. Finally, the old palace was looking more like it used to.

Prince George *clapped loudly*. Lupo gave the mice three cheers and then *howled*, "Come on George, let's go and wake everyone up!"

16
Read All About It!

Monty yawned. It had been a very slow day. He had managed to sleep right through lunch. As he rubbed what felt like sand out of his eyes he was shocked to see that the Queen was being wheeled into the room upside down on a cake trolley. He didn't move as he watched Lupo and Holly make sure that Her Majesty was perfectly comfortable on her little green sofa. Two dozen mice then got to work adjusting her royal robes and cleaning her dress, shoes and hair. One even used its own spit to polish the royal diamonds. He sat bolt upright as Burmese walked into the room with a very bubbly Prince George, *giggling* as he was gently held between her teeth.

"NOW, I SAY . . ." he started, but was interrupted by George's grandfather who was sleep-talking into his wife's left ear.

Everyone was safely back in the yellow drawing room. George's uncle was propped up by the piano next to the Duke who was ready to play "Happy Birthday".

Lupo admired the palace mice and their handy work. Holly was astonished. "That was amazing! Thank you, everyone," she said as she went about checking all the family were comfortable and ready to be woken.

The finishing touch was the Queen's birthday cake. It had taken sixteen kitchen mice and one fast asleep Morris an hour to remake the perfect cake.

Burmese eyed up the sweet carrot cake as it was manoeuvered into position. "Just one piece. No one will notice!" she pleaded.

Willow shook her head disapprovingly. "ONE BITE. THAT'S YOUR LOT!"

Burmese took a bite. It was the nicest cake she had ever tasted.

Herbert tapped his paws on the floorboards, and every mouse disappeared.

"I suppose I had better get back to the stables," said Burmese. "I can't thank you enough, everyone.

I've had a wonderful time. Come along, Ebony, I'll take you to the stables for tonight. I have a wonderful spot right in the corner for you. Matilda won't mind sharing it." With that, she helped the little Prince on to the sleeping Duchess's lap.

Ebony reluctantly followed the royal service horse out of the palace, placing one dainty little paw in front of the other while talking to herself. "ERM, I really think you should carry me. I am not used to walking. EXCUSE ME, HORSE! ANYONE?"

Burmese neighed loudly. "Oh boy, if I can get used to having Matilda in the corner of my stable, I'm sure I will eventually get used to having Ebony talking to herself the whole time! Night, everyone!" she said, galloping out into the garden.

Matilda gave Kitty a lick goodbye. Kitty wondered if her aunt would be all right sharing a stable with the ancient black cat. "Don't worry about me," said Matilda. "I don't need much space. Besides, after today's great adventure I have decided to open my own 'hotel for animals' under the palace. It's a luxury place. We'll serve only the very best salmon mousse, don't you know! I'm thinking of turning it into an ancient Egyptian themed hotel. I'm pretty sure

Ebony won't be able to resist the opportunity to run it once it's all done. Goodbye, Lupo." With that, Matilda sashayed after Burmese and Ebony.

"Noble, what are you going to do?" Lupo asked the friendly old dog.

"I think I will just see where the open road takes me. After spending thousands of years asleep it's high time I stretched my legs and had a good look around. Besides, I was never one to settle down. Goodbye, Lupo." With a bow to Prince George, he said, "My King, it has been an honour to serve you. Keep an eye out for me. I'll come and visit from time to time to check that Lupo is taking good care of you. Goodbye, everyone," said Noble as he ran out into the starry night.

As they made their way back through bookshelves of the King's Study and into the Red route tunnel that would take them all the way to Kensington Palace, the three friends yawned. It had been a very long day.

Willow stopped to thank them for their help. Vulcan was nowhere in sight. "Vulcan has a lot to answer for! I will make sure he is fully reprimanded for his terrible behaviour. Lupo, quite what we would have done without you is beyond me. The Queen owes you a great debt. I shall see that you are welcome here anytime. Farewell, Lupo."

Meanwhile, back in the living room at Buckingham Palace, the family began to wake up, and so did all the palace servants. Prince George gallantly waved his rattle in the air, enjoying the sound of the rattle's tiny bells.

The following morning the Queen's husband was in his study when there was a knock at the door. Carefully, he closed Bertie's journal and said, "Come in."

It was Tommy the footman. "Sir, you asked me to fetch the security tapes from last night," he said, putting the tapes on the desk.

"Thank you, Tommy. That will be all. Please could you make sure that I am not disturbed?" His hand rested on top of the old leather diary, fingers keen to continue exploring its dusty pages.

"Yes, sir." But Tommy didn't leave. "Is there something else, Tommy?" frowned George's great-grandfather.

"Sir, it's a bit of a mystery, sir. The servants are all

talking about it, sir."

"Talking about what, Tommy?" asked the Queen's husband sternly.

Tommy shrugged apologetically. "About what happened last night. You see, sir, none of us can remember anything between lunch and afternoon tea, sir."

"Well, I remember everything perfectly well and I can tell you, it was the biggest and best party I think this palace has ever seen. Cook must have put too much wine in your stew at lunchtime. Shouldn't worry. No harm done. All is well."

Tommy still didn't leave. "Cooking wine? Stew? Sir?"

"Yes, yes, cooking wine," said George's great grandfather, but this didn't stop the footman's curiosity. "What is it, man? Speak up!"

"Today's papers, sir. I don't suppose you have had a chance to take a look at them, sir?"

The Queen's husband shook his head. "You know I don't read the newspapers unless there is something very important in them."

Tommy unfolded a copy of *The Times*. On the front page of the "Birthday Souvenir Edition" was a picture of Her Majesty on Buckingham Palace's balcony in her big round sunglasses and royal robes riding Burmese.

Monty opened one eye, looked up from beneath the comfy lounge chair and shook his head disapprovingly at the photo of the Queen. Holly, who was resting on an old Persian rug, tried her best not to laugh out loud.

Handing back the paper, George's great-grandfather smiled knowingly. He remarked, "Like I said, Tommy, it was quite a party."

Tommy took his leave and backed out of the room, bowing as he left.

The door clicked shut, and George's great-grandfather opened Bertie's dusty journal. "Well, Bertie. Now that I have the security tapes from yesterday I shall see exactly what went on . . . though quite how I'm going to explain it all to my wife is another matter altogether."

Nanny was inspecting the little golden rattle Prince George was playing with when the Duke and Duchess walked into the Nursery. "What a pretty little rattle!" she exclaimed as she tickled the little prince's toes.

"Yes, thank you, Nanny, it was extremely generous of you," said the Duke.

The Duchess picked up the rattle and gave it to her happy son. "It really is very beautiful. Thank you."

Nanny pulled a funny face, and Prince George burst out laughing. Both Lupo and George thought that Nanny had a very funny-looking face, especially when she was confused.

"I'm sorry, your Royal Highnesses," she said, "but I didn't give Prince George the rattle!"

The Duchess looked down at the rattle in George's chubby fist. "If no one in the family gave it to him, nor anyone at Buckingham Palace, where did he get it from?"

The Duke danced around the nursery with Lupo barking at his heels. "It's a mystery! Another mystery!"

The Duke kissed his young son goodnight and dashed off. The Duchess and Nanny tucked Prince George into his cot.

Lupo watched as the Duchess walked out of the Nursery after Nanny. He could hear them chatting in the corridor. He snuggled into his blanket under the cot.

"Talking of mysteries, I had the strangest dream last night. I dreamt of a black cat sitting on the throne of England!" said the Duchess.

Nanny replied, "My grandmother would say that is an omen. Not sure it is a good one. There may be trouble ahead."

"Not sure I like the sound of that," said the Duchess, yawning loudly. "Golly, I'm tired. Right, I'm going to feed the baby before a nice long sleep. Tonight, the Duke's not getting out of the night feed! Goodnight, Nanny."

Lupo scratched the underside of the cot. "George, did you hear that? There may be trouble ahead!"

Prince George warbled. "Another baby?"

Lupo laughed and wagged his tail. "You are funny, George. *You* were a baby once and I remember just how troublesome *you* were!"

George blew a long raspberry then said, "E-pit, Lupo, E-pit! Tell me again all about E-pit!"

Lupo flicked on the tiny nursery night light and began to tell George all about Bertie's adventures in the forgotten cave and the ancient mummy cat's terrible curse. When at last George fell asleep he went to the window and looked up at the moon.

218

Kitty joined him. "That was quite some adventure, Lupo."

Looking up at the moon, he found himself thinking back to the night the Duke had first told them all about Prince Bertie's missing journals. It *had* been a terrific adventure.

"Do you want to know what I wished for when I saw the shooting star the other night?"

"Go on, then, tell me," she purred.

"That things will never change. That we will be friends for ever."

"Lupo, that's impossible," she said, smiling. "Don't you know cats and dogs can never be friends?" Together they laughed.

"He's checking up on you, no doubt," said Kitty seeing Noble standing in the middle of the private gardens beyond the nursery window.

In the soft moonlight Lupo saw Noble jumping over Kensington Gardens wall.

"Safe travels, friend," Lupo said aloud, before saying goodnight to Kitty and returning to his bed under the cot, turning several times to get comfortable. When at last he put his nose down he fell into a deep dream-filled sleep.

Tommy the footman was keen to get back to the Palace. He had a lot of silver left to polish. "That's all of it. His Royal Highness has asked that the donation remain anonymous. Got it?"

The head curator of the British Museum was flabbergasted. He hadn't seen such a collection in all his life. "Well, of course, if that is the way he would like it. But where on earth did you find it all? It's not every day the entire contents of an ancient Egyptian tomb are discovered!"

Tommy grinned. "In the old pantry, of course."

Several men finished unloading, unaware they were being watched.

"That will do," said one of the porters. Then, taking a closer look at one of the large boxes marked

"VR" he smiled with pride. "I suspect a great many people will want to see the fine ancient splendours within these crates."

As the last of them was wheeled into the back of the museum, he turned to his confused and bewildered boss. "Did you see that golden cat mask? Quite something. I could have sworn it looked directly at me with these big green eyes, when we were loading it up . . ."

"Did you say *green eyes*? How odd . . . I was dreaming about a cat last night and . . ." All of a sudden he felt quite weak. He steadied himself on a nearby box.

Tommy rushed to his side. "All this excitement has got the better of you, sir. It got the better of most of us at the Palace so you're in good company. Come on, I find that everyone always feels better after I've got them a nice cup of tea and a chocolate biscuit."

Meanwhile, the large black rat who was watching pushed Ebony forward. "GO AND GET IT NOW, whilst they are distracted. The master says he wants it before sundown."

Ebony flashed her green eyes angrily at the rat. "Claw, watch it, I was Queen once. Besides, your master doesn't have the faintest idea of the power he will wield once he's got his feathery claws on my mask. Wait here, this may take a while."

No one noticed the black cat slipping into the back entrance of the museum.

Claw pulled at his forelock, eagerly awaiting the strange cat's return and what would no doubt be a grand reward from his master at the Tower.

Turn the page for more exciting stories
from Hodder Children's Books . . .

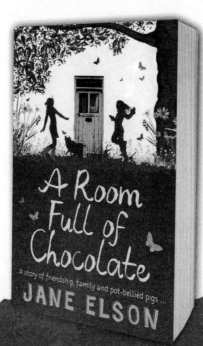

Armed with a pair of purple
rollerskates and a brain with as
many connections as there are
stars in the universe, eleven-
year-old Sesame Seade is more
than qualified to be Cambridge's
number one self-made
supersleuth. All she needs now
is a mission.

So when a student ballerina and
aspiring journalist vanishes into
thin air, some serious sleuthing
begins. Very much against her
parents' wishes, but with help
from her friends Toby and
Gemma and a conspiratorial
duck, Sesame slips into the
wings and solves the mystery of
the missing dancer.

www.hodderchildrens.co.uk

Hodder
Children's
Books

Pegasus

A MYTHICAL STALLION, A BRAVE RIDER
THE LEGEND IS BORN

*'Anyone who enjoys mythology will find much to love
in Pegasus and the Flame. Kate O'Hearn serves up a winning
mix of modern adventure and classic fantasy.'*

Rick Riordan, author of the Percy Jackson series